CW01622131

The CULLEN books by Mark Farrer
(in chronological order):

Dirty Barry

Where Seagulls Dare

Bronchial Billy

A Fistful Of Collars

Pale Ale Rider

The Good The Bad & The Rugby

The Shed Pool

Lay Misty For Me

TROUBLE WITH THE PERV

mark farrer

funny business press

TROUBLE WITH THE PERV

Published by Funny Business Press

To JT
For his brilliant covers.

This is a work of fiction.
Names, characters, places and incidents either are products of the author's imagination or are used fictitiously.
Any resemblance to actual events or locales or persons, living or dead, is entirely coincidental.
Except for Big Paul.

CONTENTS

ONE

TWO

THREE

FOUR

FIVE

SIX

SEVEN

EIGHT

POSTSCRIPT

AUTHOR'S NOTE

ONE

"Good, good, good, good... morning!" Charles Bryce breezed into Lingerie like a brush with new bristles, a sharp ring to his voice and a toothpaste-ad grin.

Joanne Montague clutched a handful of baby pink lace 36C's *(New In, only £24.99)* to her chest in alarm.

"Dear Lord, I thought we were being burgled!"

Blinking away shock at the sight of the store's proprietor beaming at her like a lunatic on a secret mission, she managed to transform her features into a welcoming smile, flecks of coral pink lipstick (*Only two left at £4.99*) showing on her teeth.

"Now Joanne. *Thou shalt not take the name of the Lord, thy God, in vain.* Exodus 20, verse 7."

"No, of course... I... You know I didn't-"

"Only joking, Ms Montague. Only joking!" Charles sent her an exaggerated wink, delivered to reassure but received as more of a salacious tic. He lifted himself up onto the balls of his feet, flexing up and down, like some headmaster waiting for assembly to quieten. That smug, self-satisfied look on his face, hands clasped behind his back - Joanne knew she wasn't alone in finding it more than a little disturbing.

"Oh. Oh thank goodness." Joanne gave her a head a little shake and put one hand to her throat, straightening the chunky stone necklace there (*Last Season's, newly reduced to £14.99*). It wouldn't have been the first time she had been reprimanded for some absurd breach of his religious protocol, the rules with which she was supremely unfamiliar. He may be a Jehovah's Witness of long standing but she had no time for religious claptrap or mumbo-jumbo.

"You are bright and breezy this morning, Mr Bryce, I must say. Would you like a cup of tea?"

"Yes, indeed!" Charles chirped, striding on past her deeper into the Ladies' section, wispy garments swaying on their hangers as he passed. "But stay there my good lady. Let me be mother."

"Oh. How thoughtful. Thank you."

"Not at all. Not at all. *Give, and it will be given to you.* Luke 6, verse 38." He waved over his shoulder.

"Well, thank you all the same." Joanne called at his back.

He paused at the entrance to the stockroom and turned.

"Besides... beautiful morning like this, brings the customers out early. You can't be serving them if you're putting the kettle on, can you?" He disappeared through the curtain with a flourish, a magician about to astound his audience with nothing so mundane as a cup of tea.

Joanne pursed her lips and exhaled loudly and slowly. The Creep was early today.

Big Paul was picking stuff off surfaces, peering under styrofoam boxes and rooting through assorted detritus in his living room, searching for a tape measure. Ant, one of his Jack Russells, lay in the watery sunshine at the open doorway chewing an old piece of wood; the other one,

Dec, was chasing Paul around the room as he went, skipping and barking, enjoying his game of Hide and Seek. Dec barked happily again and Paul stared at him.

"You're no help."

A shadow appeared at his window and Paul looked up in alarm, his search rudely interrupted.

"Blimey! Who are you and what have you done with Mungo?"

Cullen, who had poked his head around the back door to Paul's cabin, scowled at the unwanted use of his Christian name. Paul took a nervous moment, regretting his hasty witticism, and looked his old friend up and down.

Whichever way you put it, Cullen looked a bit of a mess, but unusually so today because he was hatless. The battered leather cowboy hat, forever clamped to his head, slightly squashing his ears, slightly scrunching his curls so that they played hide-and-seek untidily around the brim. Even his face looked like it was infected by the scuffed leathery appearance, his complexion often merging into his hat if the light was right. Or wrong, your choice.

"Cup of tea?" Paul said, making a peace offering.

"How many times- ?"

"Oh, yeah. Soz. No tea, gotcha." Paul scratched his own untidy stubble. "Well, um, you kinda got me there then 'cos I don't have much else to offer. Apart from beer which - I know!" Paul stuck an upraised palm out before Cullen issued another disapproving, weary shake of the head.

"It may surprise you to know..." Cullen rubbed one eye with a dirty finger. "That I do not frequent your establishment merely for the libations on offer."

"You wot?"

Cullen removed his finger and sighed. "I don't come

here for the drinks."

"Yeah. And I think *frequent* is putting it a bit strong 'n all. Maybe *infrequent* - is that a verb too?"

"No idea." Cullen leant back on the handrail around the decking. It gave somewhat alarmingly.

"Er... yeah... don't, um, put your full weight on that or anythin'. Work in progress you might say."

"Twas ever thus." Cullen let go of the handrail and let his eyes roam carelessly over Paul's cabin in front of him. It was constructed entirely of wood, and a motley selection of it at that. Here and there, loose patches of untrimmed tarpaulin fluttered in the breeze. Occupying a jaunty position on a hillside overlooking a bright burn, steps led down to it from a stony path. It possessed a sloping front garden abandoned to long grass, and a large deck protruding out at the rear, the space below which was stuffed with logs, bin bags and more than one rusty wheelbarrow. A jaundiced eye might have expected a mangy sofa to be sitting in his front yard, or perhaps an old banger up on blocks. But even Paul had standards. He was above white trash - just; he was white clutter.

"You know, anyone who didn't know you - looking at this - could tell you were a joiner who struggles with alcohol."

"I don't struggle." Paul was offended. "I'm pretty good at it."

"Really." Cullen's eyes roamed once more over the structure. "What did you make when you were last drunk?"

"About £25 an hour, actually. Not that that's any of your business." Paul raised his eyebrows. "And, speaking of business: state yours."

Cullen snapped out of his reverie. "May I use your

facilities?"

"You mean: the bog?"

"If you must, yes."

"Well, if you must, yes." Paul thumbed vaguely behind him and watched Cullen step gingerly over Ant, still lying in the doorway, and head past. "Just don't flush it yet. Not until I've found that blasted tape measure." Paul was one of those people who review their bowel movements like a VAR decision. He put the kettle onto boil while he continued his search.

Cullen returned, tripping over a box as he made his way back out into fresher air. Paul followed him, puffing slightly. He was large man with a build not unlike a huge, muscular thumb which had recently taken to carrying an Atlas Stone under its sweatshirt. He slumped into a deckchair and eyed his friend again, the sight of Cullen's bare head causing him some cognitive dissonance.

"You need a hat."

"I know. Don't suppose you-?"

"Not big on headgear myself. Ruins my look."

"What look is that, exactly?"

"Cool... well-maintained... obtainable. The ladies like olive skin and peach fuzz." Paul stroked a giant mitt across his head, a shining dome covered with short black hair, like moleskin. "Besides, hats make me sweat. Fifteen minutes and I'm dripping like a knackered fridge."

"Which would be neither cool nor well-maintained."

"My point. Exactly."

Cullen paused for a moment. "Obtainable. So, you and Shirley are still not...?"

"Do not mention her name in my presence." Paul's face darkened. "She and I are no longer a thing. I am free to date who I want. And eat pies."

"That what you had for lunch is it?" Cullen indicated the nasty stain down the front of Paul's sweatshirt. At least the stain was fresh.

"That's just..." Paul searched for a word. "Garnish."

"Yes. Nothing says cool, well-maintained and obtainable like garnish all down your front."

Paul said nothing but his eyes burnt black under his brows. His friend eyed him suspiciously.

"You eating properly?"

Paul slapped his belly proudly. "What do you think?"

"I said properly, not enormously."

"Same thing."

"No. It really isn't." Cullen sighed, the sound punctuating the still morning. "She's a good cook, isn't she?"

"Are you deaf?"

"I didn't use her name."

Paul pouted. "I can cook."

"Yeah?"

"Been learning. Off Davy."

"Christ."

"Just... well, don't have the facilities." Paul waved airily behind him at his cabin. "Kitchen's still a..."

"Work in progress?"

"'Xactly."

"Speaking of pies, I hear Greggs have got a new attraction. A man."

"Not interested."

"The queues are down the High Street."

"Don't care."

Cullen watched in silence, while Paul busily dug at some imperfection in his deckchair with a massive fingernail.

"Have you met him?"

"None of my business."

"I bet she's pleased. Profits must be up."

"Not bothered."

"So you said."

Paul turned to frown at Cullen. "Meaning?"

"Nothing."

Paul gritted his teeth. "Read my lips: I. Am not. Interested."

"Please yourself." Cullen rose, a decision of some sort clearly made.

"Where you off to?"

"To buy a hat." He zipped up his coat and strode off Paul's decking.

"But you never told me why you were here!"

Paul's word vanished in the empty air and he was left staring at the space where Cullen had been. He sat contemplating the early morning stillness. You couldn't beat sitting outside in the fresh air, on your own balcony, the birds singing and a whole day of idleness ahead of you to enjoy it in.

The kettle in the kitchen started to whistle and, as if on cue, Paul's stomach rumbled. He sighed, struggled out of his deckchair and shuffled into his kitchen. The sink was plumbed in and working, thanks to the water supply he had purloined from his neighbour who ran an unofficial pipeline down the hillside from a small spring hidden in the trees. There were a few cabinets Paul had acquired from a skip when someone had been throwing out their old kitchen, and a butcher's block he'd got from Davy after helping him in the pub cellar one time.

The whole ramshackle place, though, was brightened by some feminine touches which she-who-must-not-be-named had artfully applied during their relationship so that she could better tolerate what she had called *the conditions.* He remembered screwing up his face, not understanding what she was referring to - an expression she had responded to with "it's a bit like waking up every morning to find yourself in a famine relief camp."

Paul smiled at the memory and his stomach rumbled again.

God, he could just go a giant sausage roll right now.

He stood and, as one, Ant and Dec raced towards him, their claws skittering on the shiny floor.

"Later, fellas." Paul said. "You wait here. I'll bring you something back."

His pets watched, emitting tiny whimpers, as he marched out into the sunshine without them.

Charles Aloysius Bryce had no idea he was referred to as The Creep. Had no idea, in fact, that he was disliked by anyone since, well, how could anyone dislike *him*? He was smooth, sleek and superior, driven by sanctimony, self-righteousness, and entitlement. Powerfully driven. In fact, if you have a moment, he had an engine that could deliver superiority throughout its entire range, boasting five hundred percent certainty at peak revs, reaching twelve definitelys per hour, fifty no-doubt-about-its to the gallon.

However, like any engine, unfortunately he polluted, emitting a foul exhaust: smarm. But being a scion of one of the town's most-beloved families, a proud freeman of the burgh, he had no idea of the extent of the smarm that trailed behind him. It was but the merest hint of discolouration in his rear-view mirror - and Charles had no time for looking back. His eyes were locked on the road ahead as he powered ever onward, supercharged by his own entitlement. Meanwhile, those poor unfortunates standing by the wayside, found themselves covered in it, getting it on their clothes, in their hair, their eyes, their mouths. Choking on it, streaming tears, as they tried in vain to evade the all-pervasive, icky, oozy, oleaginous, noxious... smarm.

Daily he would cruise around his estate: Bryce & Sons. A small department store and landmark in the town, a physical embodiment of heritage, nobility, and civic pride. And not just civic pride - *his* pride, *his* joy, *his* domain, *his* fiefdom.

It stood on a corner plot in an old Victorian pile, all stairways and odd windows, turrets and crenellations. A building with a maze-like interior, folded in on itself like some Escher tesseract. Endless narrow corridors led to small flights of steps, and right-angled landings fed into small rooms from which there would be another exit. But, like a USB stick that wouldn't go into its socket until you had tried it the right way up, the wrong way up and then the right way up again, you had to enter the space, circle it, circle it again and then, just as you were on the point of leaving the way you came in, you would find a magical new doorway leading to another space, on a slightly different level naturally, which beckoned you on until you were lost in the belly of the building. Your only hope of escape was to ask an assistant for directions and then they had you. Leaving Bryce's without a purchase was impossible. Somewhere on a distant hilltop there was said to be a wise old man who had managed it, and you could beat a path to his door to ask him how he did it, but he had taken a vow of silence and you would find your journey wasted.

Charles threw the kettle under the tap and put it on to

boil and then crept back to the curtain, peeking out to see Joanne helping some old lady holding a nightie up to the window. Reassured he wouldn't be disturbed, he moved nimbly over to an empty bookcase against a wall and lifted it deftly out of the way to reveal a small panel cut into the plasterboard. He bent down and peeped into the cavity - the video camera was still there and its recording light was on.

Content, he replaced the bookcase and waited for the kettle. Carrying two mugs of tea on a tray he pushed through the curtain to see Joanne already ringing up a sale at the counter. Smiling, he put the tray of teas down. The tea could wait - business was business, after all.

"Do not neglect to do good and to share what you have, for such sacrifices are pleasing to God. Hebrews 13, verse 16." He said to himself, as he turned and strode off to check on his other cameras.

"Excuse me, could I have a wod with you about Thee Lod?"

Standing alone on the freezing street corner, Blessing Mnangwa was shaking with cold. The old women in rainhoods chicaned away from her as she tried to catch their eye. They were swift on their feet when they wanted to be, Blessing saw. She looked after them as they hurried down the High Street. It was unremarkable in many ways - a typical grey scene, rain-soaked paving stones and wet tarmac, cars parked along both sides of the street, pedestrians bent into the wind striking out earnestly for shelter.

Unremarkable maybe, but not to her. She hugged her thin outfit to her and tried to smile. This was a world away from everything she had known. Back in her native Ghana, children flew across baked earth in bare feet, not so much roads as uneven stretches of red clay between flimsy huts on one side and an open sewer on the other. Passing vehicles, most decades old, jounced and rattled up and down on this cratered surface more like the Somme than a High Street. Horns sounded gaily, music blared and people shouted; everywhere was a riot of colour and sound, sunshine and hot, choking dust.

Contrast that with this cold, muted, drab drizzle of a Scottish Borders morning. Standing proudly in her Ghanaian national dress, she looked like a peacock in a chiller cabinet, trying to hand religious pamphlets to heads-down folk who would no more take something from a black stranger than they would kill their first-born.

"The wod of our blessed Lod Jeez U?"

The rain spattered her head-dress, a spectacular towering construction of garish material which tottered on her like a technicolour turban. Ghanaian women traditionally balanced - well, everything - on their heads and walked fully laden from place to place, often bearing a considerable weight (gallon jugs of water perhaps, huge bowls of glistening fruit to market, stacks of clean crockery being taken home from the river). Fully laden, they still managed the smooth, sashaying grace of a cheetah retreating into the shade.

Here the Scottish women, mostly elderly, tugged begrudgingly on wheeled tartan trolleys, lugging them behind them like ungrateful children being taken to a great Aunt for a Sunday treat.

In Ghana battered folding umbrellas were used as parasols to protect you from the beating sun; here they acted as shields, held at arm's length into the teeth of the wind, as their owners vainly tried to persuade the rain to pick on someone else.

There, neon-coloured togas and skirts dazzled over flimsy sandals and leather thongs as feet scuffed through the dust and dirt; here it was all headscarves and raincoats, fleeces and kagools, their supposedly-vivid colours bleeding into a muted colour palette in the grey light.

She had swapped one for the other and, standing here as the rain stung her bare legs and trickled down between her toes she sighed, thanking her Pastor, Isaiah, for bringing her to this place where his destiny lay and his holy mission could be fulfilled.

She was, as Isaiah often told her, doing *Thee Lod's Wok.*

TWO

"Any sort of hat in particular?" Joanne asked the tramp. Ordinarily she would have simply stonewalled and directed him downstairs to Menswear but here came The Creep breathing down her neck bearing tea on a tray - finally. In front of him, it was best she establish who the hat was for first.

Her boss placed the tea down next to her and then leant ever-so-slightly forward, imperceptibly sniffing the air, earning a narrow-eyed look from this stranger. The man was tall and gaunt, unruly hair curled shaggily on his head and around his ears. It needed a cut and it wasn't exactly clean. Standing there, scruffy in a torn, stained waterproof jacket with combat pants and boots smelling of fresh mud, he drew a stark contrast to Charles Bryce with his smooth middle-aged skin, double-breasted suit, expensive shoes, a handkerchief in his top pocket and the odour of sandalwood aftershave.

"Have you tried the Charity Shop?" Charles sneered, moving forwards onto his toes, perhaps in anticipation of some trouble. The man squinted at him, disdain and annoyance shooting across the gap between them. He looked Charles up and down, spending a split-second longer than seemed necessary on his lapels, then ignored him and answered Joanne.

"A warm one." His eyes were like flints.

"Is it for yourself, Sir?" The difficulty with which her boss dragged out the final word was almost visible in the air.

"And you are?" His eyes once more came to rest on Charles' lapels and then stole upwards.

Charles stiffened and rested back on his heels, suddenly wary. He tried an appeasing smile and raised his mug to his lips. "I am the proprietor of this establishment."

The tramp nodded to the tray. "Who brings tea?"

"*Give and it will be given unto you.* Luke 6, verse 38." Charles smarmed.

"Would you like some?" Joanne offered boldly. Charles' eyes bulged at her suggestion.

"Just a hat."

"Yes. Well, we have several, in *Menswear.*" Charles put his tea down on the counter and stepped out onto the shop floor, owning the space.

"Couldn't find it. Place is a warren." The man looked around, somewhat uncomfortably, at the bras and panties hanging from the rails.

"Yes." Charles gave the tightest smile. "It is an intricate building. Gives it charm, though, don't you think?"

The look on the man's face said that he clearly didn't agree.

"Would you care to follow me?"

"No. Thank you."

Joanne stifled a smirk as she saw The Creep's eyes widen in surprise. The tramp looked into her eyes. "Perhaps *you* could..."

"Of course, Sir." Agreed Joanne. It wasn't often anyone stood up to The Creep. She liked the cut of this man's jib. She looked over to her boss. "If you wouldn't mind holding the fort here, Mr Bryce, while I take this gentleman to Menswear?"

"Of course, of course." Charles flashed a smile, teeth clenched, facial muscles twitching and watched, fingers crossed, as Joanne led the tramp with his backpack through the ranks of closely packed rails and display stands out of sight.

When she got downstairs, Joanne ran her hands over a rotating stand of various beanies and flat caps, talking animatedly with her back to the man assuming he was right behind her.

"Would you like to try one on?"

Getting no response, she turned and saw him standing a yard or two away, seemingly unwilling to come closer.

"Oh. Um, how about this one?" She held up a merino wool beanie in a beautiful prussian blue, a discreet logo embroidered at the front.

"How much?"

"£29.99." She thought she heard him gulp. "It'll keep you lovely and warm. It's merino wool. Wicks wonderfully as well."

He cast an undiscerning eye over the other hats in the display and nodded at a fairly awful hat bearing a REDUCED sticker. It was tightly woven wool in a colour that she could only describe as sewage-outlet brown with a wide neon orange stripe. It made a very nasty double-act with his lime green waterproof.

"How much is that?"

"£7.99" She tried to smile approvingly. "A bargain, really. Would you like to try it on?"

"I don't think that will be necessary." From nowhere, The Creep had reappeared at her shoulder, authority in his voice. Out of the corner of his mouth she heard him say: "If he tries it on and doesn't like it, we'll never get the smell out."

"I'll take it." The man dug into a trouser pocket and threw some coins onto the glass counter by way of an answer and The Creep chanced another furtive sniff as he did so. Joanne scooped up the coins and bustled back to the till.

"Would you like a bag?" Her boss made this sound almost like a threat. But the man wordlessly jammed the hat onto his head, sticker and all, and giving The Creep one last glare, swept out through the door.

"You do realise we don't accept returns!" Charles called after him as the bell over the door rang out through the sudden stillness inside the shop. Joanne stood stiffly, The Creep inappropriately close beside her, as together they watched the tramp vanish up the High Street.

"Maybe he's colour-blind." Joanne sighed.

"Maybe he just doesn't care. Who needs fashion-sense when you sleep in doorways and don't know where your next can of Stella is going to come from?"

"At least it'll keep him warm."

"Warm." He scoffed. "Not the longest list of criteria when looking for a hat."

Joanne tried to block him out as he muttered more insults, waiting a beat or two until she retreated back upstairs to lingerie.

"Yes, ladies. How can I help you?"

Fetch me a bucket, thought Paul. Three places back in the queue, just inside Greggs' front door, he watched as this sparkly, perma-tanned smoothie flashed his teeth, bright blue eyes twinkling at the gaggle of old dears who were cooing and giggling like moonstruck schoolgirls.

What the hell was someone like this doing serving in Greggs? He looked like he should be working a Vegas residency, not shovelling sticky buns into the grateful mitts of the town's wrinklies.

Paul shifted his weight onto the other foot and looked over everyone's head towards the window of the back office. She-who-must-not-be-named had had it reglazed using some kind of striped one-way mirror glass so you thought you could see in but were never sure, and what appeared to be a shadow moving behind the glass could just as well be a fleeting reflection from a passer-by on the High Street. This wasn't the first time he'd tried - and failed - to see if she was in.

"Yes, Sir?"

He had reached the front of the queue and the twinkling, perfect-skinned, full head-of-hair was looking expectantly at him and it was just so incongruous - like being asked your inside leg by a young Liberace. Without the candelabra.

"Sausage roll." Paul blinked, dazzled by the headlights of the man's teeth. Is this what *she* liked, this fakery? "Three."

"In separate bags, Sir?"

"Um, what?"

"Would you like them in the same bag or separate bags?"

"Same." Paul screwed his face up at this weird idea, almost forgetting himself. He nodded at the office window. "Is Shir-, the manager? Is she in?"

"I am the manager, Sir."

"No, you're not."

"I am today." He flashed his teeth again, so bright they could cure cataracts. "Shirley's away on a training course.

I'm acting manager."

Paul thought he heard a strange cough from over the man's shoulder and, when he looked, he saw a slim blonde girl with a sneer on her face quickly turn away and busy herself with a cloth. He turned his attention back to this fake show pony.

"Is there anything else I can help you with at all?"

"What? Oh, um, No. Just the sausage rolls, ta."

He sleepwalked out of the shop and plunged his hand into the hot greasy bag, the fragrance of whatever-the-hell-the-filling-was rose to his nostrils, brightening his eyes and rousing his saliva - like Gollum sniffing out the *precious*. Fortifying himself, he crossed the road and strode purposefully towards the Lamb & Flag, strewing flecks of puff pastry behind him as he went.

"What the devil?"

Charles blinked hard, twice, to make sure his eyes were not deceiving him. A flamboyant figure, dressed all in white wearing a bright purple dog collar, was pronouncing loudly out across the street, pointing at the Mercat Cross in the middle of the road, his white teeth and eyes flashing in the sunshine. The man was, Charles gulped, black.

Pedestrians were stopping to watch and listen and traffic was slowing to a crawl as it passed. Through the window came the sound of a sing-song baritone, booming sufficiently to make the pane glass reverberate. All Charles could make out in terms of actual words were frequent, heavily-accented mentions of *Thee Lod*. This was the last straw.

It wasn't bad enough that he had to deal with vagrants stinking up his shop but here, in broad daylight, in front of his store, was - what? A Pentecostalist? An Evangelical? Some blaspheming, Godforsaken backwater nonsense masquerading as legitimate faith from the third world.

He spun on his feet and flew out of the door, shop doorbell clanging as he did so.

"You there! Hey, you there! Stop that right now!"

The preacher either didn't hear him or chose not to, but carried on beseeching the town to hear the word of *Thee Lod.* A car beeped its horn and a few locals, recognising Charles, hurriedly lowered their heads and scurried away. Whereas outside the Lamb & Flag, a few hardy smokers nudged each other with a grin and called inside to their pals to come and watch the upcoming entertainment. Charles caught them out of the corner of his eye and cursed under his breath.

"You, I say! What do you think you're playing at?"

He scooted across the road onto the large traffic island on which stood the town's Mercat Cross and confronted this peacocking preacher close up.

"Playing?" The black man greeted him with a massive grin, a vast expanse of enamel surrounding a large pink tongue. "My friend, I am not playing! I am doing the work of Thee Lod." He turned back to the growing audience. "Our Lod Jesu, in whose Blessed name-"

"You are doing no such thing. Get away, now! Go back to... wherever you're from and preach in your own town, not mine."

"Yours? Yours?" The preacher crowed, still beaming. "You own this town?"

"Very much so." Charles spat through gritted teeth. "Do you see the name on that building there?" He pointed at his own shop.

"Bryce?" The preacher's smile never left his face. "You

are Mister Bryce?"

"Yes. Yes, I am. And my family have -"

"You put your name on a building and proclaim it yours?" The preacher turned to his audience once again. "Pride is a sin. A deadly sin. Thee Lod opposes thee proud, and gives grace to thee humble."

Charles's eyes bulged and he shook an angry finger in the preacher's face.

"Don't you lecture me. You come here with your phony God and your-"

"Thee Lod is no phony!" The preacher brought out a Bible and brandished it aloft. "His words guide me, His Father protects me, and the Holy Spirit is within me. In the name of Thee Father, -"

"Don't you dare!" Charles couldn't stop himself from reaching out and grabbing the preacher's book. Together, the pair wrestled like a couple of porcupines over a prize - delicately, both desiring victory but neither wanting to really get hurt in the process. The sound of sarcastic cheering and encouragement drifted over from the Lamb & Flag.

Charles, having abandoned all that remained of his pride in allowing himself to get engaged in a physical tussle, now found that this preacher, being a younger man, was also more powerful than he had expected. One didn't expect a man of the cloth - no matter which material it was cut from - to have the musculature of a boxer. The preacher, little by little, was bending him against his will, twisting his arm as Charles failed to keep a grasp on the bible they were wrestling over. He found himself bent almost double, his right arm wrenched awkwardly upwards as his opponent overcame him, his eyes cast down onto the pavement. He was about to give one last almighty heave when into his vision stepped first one, then two, beautiful feet. A woman's feet. A black woman's feet. Wearing dainty silver sandals which sparkled against the darkness of her skin, with perfect toenails painted the palest porcelain pink.

Charles lost focus on his tussle and froze, mesmerized by this erotic sight. Eyes still cast down on the pavement he no longer heard the preacher, declaring proudly and holding the bible aloft in victory; no longer felt the eyes of the crowd on him or the warmth of the day; no longer felt himself a spectacle on the High Street outside his own store.

Winded he slowly stood, his eyes rising up to take in the full extent of this woman's dress, clad as she was head-to-foot in a toga-style assembly of the most vibrant colours and patterns, a towering headdress making her look eight feet tall. She was young, no more than twenty or so he would guess, and exceedingly pretty with velvet eyes and a sweet, round face. Dusting down the preacher's suit with her hands, stroking his hair, checking he was okay, all focus was on her colleague, and she never even glanced at Charles.

"Isaiah! My word, Isaiah. Are you alright?"

"I am fine." The preacher replied, brushing aside her ministrations. "And you, Sir!"

Charles stood silently, swallowing, taking his eyes from this vision only to narrow them at the preacher.

"You, Sir - go back to your precious building, thee house of Bryce! I shall go to thee House of Thee Lod and praise Him, and His Father and thee Holy Spirit, for saving me and showing His children-" Here he swept his hands over the slowly disbanding crowd that had gathered, been entertained and were now no longer interested. "His children, thee way of thee righteous."

Charles, was torn. He wanted to hide from the embarrassment of making a fool of himself in front of the town; he wanted to shout down this heathen and correct the lies and slander he was broadcasting; but most of all he wanted to feast his eyes on this wondrous black goddess and her fantastic feet.

From outside the pub a leery voice called. "Never mind, Charlie boy! Saved by the belle!" This stirred him into action. Realising the tragi-comic figure he cut, he did his best to raise his chin and stride back towards his shop. Crossing the road he spied his entire staff, who up until this point had all had their faces pressed hard against the window watching this bizarre encounter, scurry out of sight into the darkness of the store like rabbits diving for their burrows.

He closed the shop door behind him and stood alone in the entrance, shaking his head sadly. This man's blaspheming church was defiling the name of the Lord by declaring him to be only one part of a Trinity.

The image of perfect pink nail polish clouded his view.

The Jehovah's Witness creed was very clear on this subject - crystal - since their very faith required them to believe that the Trinity did not exist. There was only one God and he was all supreme. Jesus may have been His son and the Holy Spirit some particular instance of His manifestation but to say that Our Lord was only one among three equals?

Perfect black toes peeped through elegant silver sandals. He could almost smell perfume.

And this man also revelled in the Christian name of Isaiah! Isaiah, the prophet? Whose name literally translated meant *God is Salvation.* What heresy was this?

He could see the arch of her instep, the tightened tendons on the bridge of her foot, the delicate bones at her ankle.

This wasn't mere indignity or insult. The Jehovah's Witness monthly magazine, *The Watchtower*, was named to reflect the battle that was needed to be waged, every day and every night, against the heathen and the unbeliever and the inconstant.

He imagined undoing the clasp of her sandal. Slipping her cool, slender foot into his warm, quivering hand.

And here, on his own doorstep, was the very Satan himself. Inviting him into battle.

He brought her foot up to his nose and inhaled her fragrance. A tremor shivered through him.

This wasn't a battle; this was war.

"It's quite simple, you ask me." Davy declared, expelling a much-needed drag from a cigarette into the bright spring air.

"I'm not asking you."

"Seen it all before, Beep. I'm an expert in all this. Do you know how many customers have confided in me over the years?"

"Don't care."

"Loads."

"I don't care."

Paul was glum, despite holding a pint in the morning sunshine outside the Lamb & Flag. Out down the High Street he could see a crowd forming and some ruckus occurring. He craned his neck whilst supping his pint while the landlord continued to harry him.

"It's obvious to me, is all I'm saying. Clear as day." Davy persisted.

"Really."

"Aye. Simply put-"

"I'll simply put you if you don't shut up."

"You're jealous."

"I'm not."

"You are. That's what this is. She's got this new orange fella and your nose is all out of joint."

"No."

"And you go into Greggs to try and provoke her into talking to you. And she won't."

"Nope."

"She came in here a few times looking for you. But you hid from her and now she's stopped bothering."

"Shut up."

"So you need to try harder." Davy sniffed. "Or give up, your choice."

"Why should I? I mean, why is it on me? She's the one owes me an apology."

"You were the one fucked up first. Maybe she's just getting her own back? Or maybe she just doesn't have the same feelings for you anymore? Who knows." Davy took another drag. "Plus, you're the bloke. 'Course it's on you."

The disturbance on the High Street was generating more interest and there was a proper commotion growing. Through a gap in the crowd, Paul and Davy could see what appeared to be a black vicar in a white suit shouting at another bloke in a suit. They looked on keenly as they continued their conversation.

"It's not right."

"No, it's just the way it is."

"It's not right and it's not fair."

"No." Agreed Davy. "And neither is that vicar's left leg."

"What do you think they're doing?" Paul's gaze was drawn to the sudden appearance of a young black woman in a colourful outfit, coming to the aide of the shouting vicar.

"Religion innit? All conflict stems from religion. This is just it in microcosm." Davy gestured with his cigarette at the spectacle of the two men wrestling. "See what you got there is a spectacle. Everyone loves a spectacle. It's exciting. Arousing. Gets the blood up."

"Aye." Paul said, absently, unable to take his eyes off the woman.

"That's what you should do, actually. Get Shirley's blood up."

"Hmm?"

"Get her blood up. Then you'll know whether she's still interested in you or not, won't you? This orange bloke has got your blood up - get hers up!"

"How do I do that then?"

"Do what she's done - get yourself someone new."

"I don't want someone new." Paul mused, still distracted.

"Well, pretend then. Find someone, parade round with her on your arm in front of Shirley, see what happens. Get her blood up!"

"You reckon?"

"And the greater the apparent threat to her, the more she'll get aroused. Spectacle, you see?"

Paul's eyes were locked on the young woman as Davy's word wormed their way into his brain. He tried to make sense of them.

"Spectacle. Threat. Aroused." He muttered, absently.

"Exactly." Davy threw his cigarette on the floor and stubbed it out with his foot. "But whatever you do, can you just get on and do it, for God's sake. I don't want to have to keep hearing about all this bleedin' playground bollocks. Pair of you need to grow up, you're not twelve."

"Spectacle. Threat. Aroused." And Paul's eyes never left the beautiful young black woman as she led the vicar away down North Street.

THREE

Shirley's mind wandered as Trevor droned away in front of the whiteboard, scratching his head whenever he had to contemplate his notes - a process which caused flecks of dandruff and scalp to fall free and get caught in the shaft of reticent sunlight coming in from the large dirty windows. She pondered her instructor's shirt which bore a pale stripe, visible only when the light shone at a certain angle. Unfortunately, at said angle, it also revealed the contours of his pot belly which were giving his white buttons so much trouble. The shirt, clearly only poly-cotton, was always going to struggle to contain his stomach, always going to fail to conceal it.

She unconsciously shook her head in disappointment. Shirley had inherited from her mother a sort of snobbishness when it came to materials which directly touched your skin. Always had to be pure, 100% of whatever they were, if it touched your skin. Knickers, stockings, blouses, scarves - had to be either cotton, silk or wool. Never, ever nylon or anything man-made touching you. Dear Lord, never mind the material! Her mother hadn't trusted any man (other than Shirley's father) to touch her skin - and sometimes even that had been a trial for her.

Trevor's trousers (100% polyester, Shirley sniffed) slung below his belly like some sulking tightrope walker waiting to be promoted to the big time - the day would come when they would be asked to traverse this great expanse, but not today; today they sulked in the shade of this proud promontory, awaiting the spotlight.

She looked up from his belly to his mouth and tried to focus on its output - something about team-building filtered through to her and she frantically tried to snap back into the moment and pay attention.

This was just the sort of thing she needed, not the rest of this management guff he was spouting. She looked down at her pad and the agenda item she had underlined - *Personnel Targets and Engagement.* It made it sound as if they were going to be taught about advanced battlefield technology, laser-guided drones which would zone in on staff and take them out, AI smartbombs which would detonate if productivity fell below a certain level, dirty grenades which would scatter shrapnel and other skin-shredding contents over a discrete area if an employee failed to change the till roll without a queue forming.

But no, it wasn't anything so dramatic, it was mostly management fluff - or, as Paul would call it: *wank*. She smiled at the thought of the conversation she might have with him about it, at the end of the day, coming home to unburden herself and have him listen patiently and empathise, in his own way, by either brushing it off as a minor inconvenience or imparting some piece of gleaned wisdom - usually gleaned from that unreliable landlord, Davy - which would no doubt take the shine off the ball of each delivered gem.

But that conversation wasn't going to occur now, was it? Not tonight or any night because Paul had slipped out of her life and, she gritted her teeth, she had let him. Dumped, her mother had said, causing Shirley to grit her teeth again. She'd been doing a lot of that lately. It had taken her a week or so to drum up the courage to tell her mother, time she had spent hoping to get hold of Paul. But she had failed in that as well and one Sunday, feeling sorry for herself, she had confessed this failure to her mother who had pounced on it and then devoured the details, noisily and eagerly, only to then shit out the nub of the problem (Shirley's problem) for the benefit of Shirley's hindsight.

Thanks, Mum.

You're welcome, Shirl.

She bit her lip, quickly scanning the other attendees in the classroom, checking to make sure she had not revealed any of her inner workings. Actually they weren't attendees, they were *management cadets*. Shirley found it more than a little degrading, given her age, to be called a *cadet* by Trevor. Cadets were teenagers or, at least, inexperienced youngsters in need of schooling: Traci was a cadet, not Shirley. Shirley was an old dog being reluctantly taught new tricks by this pot-bellied Gandalf that Paul would have called *a wazzock*.

But she had better listen to this wazzock because when it came to team building, Shirley was very much in need of some pointers. With the introduction of Alasdair to her cosy shop crew she had seemingly thrown a cat amongst the pigeons and now, whereas the customers had never been happier, the staff were at each others' throats.

Alasdair was the new kid on the block. She had hired him on the spot, within seconds of seeing him, and while she realised that this was not a tremendous example of Greggs recruitment policy she'd had no regrets - for a while. Alasdair was a gleaming, shining Adonis with perfect skin and perfect teeth, charm and poise and buckets of experience and expertise. He was God's gift to retail and Shirley couldn't believe he had fallen into her lap. Their takings went through the roof once word got around that Greggs had a heartthrob behind the counter. Days when Alasdair took a shift saw queues down the High Street; days when he wasn't there were like Sundays which spun slowly, achingly, by. It wouldn't have surprised Shirley if they hadn't printed his shift patterns in the local paper so that everyone would know when to turn up.

She had tried to see only the positives - it wasn't as if takings were down when Alasdair was absent; it was normal, everyday, previously satisfactory business. It was just that, when he was there, business rocketed and so these periods of normality started to look like scalding, barren deserts in a landscape of shimmering peaks.

But the negatives had not taken long to emerge. Because that wasn't Traci's way. Traci was always willing to help out, as long as that help involved chipping in with some sarcastic remark or dismissive gesture to show that, at this time, she was, regrettably, unable to bring herself to give a toss. Traci was young and Greggs was her first employment since leaving school - Shirley couldn't bring herself to say "finishing" as this would have been stretching the truth somewhat. She found a Saturday job at Greggs, under previous store management, and by the time Shirley had herself joined Greggs, Traci was no longer a pain in the arse Saturdays only, she had progressed to full-time pain in the arse. Perhaps she had a talent for something after all?

She certainly had a tongue and a face for it. Best described as sullen, Traci's face constantly displayed this curious combination of expressionless boredom and lack of desire to relieve it. Beneath huge eyebrows which looked like they'd been tattooed on, she was shockingly over made-up for - well, anything that didn't involve excessive alcohol and insufficient light. Everything was too much trouble for her and nothing was her responsibility. On the scale of "pleased to be of service" Traci sat somewhere between dead-eyed insolence and not-my-problem. But she was Shirley's problem because Alasdair's arrival had made Traci's attitude ten times worse.

Or at least thrown it into sharper relief.

"Traci, could you please check the sugar shakers?"

Traci would slope off and return wordlessly some moments later. When Shirley then found a shaker empty, she would call:

"Traci? I asked you to check the shakers!"

"I did."

"Well, this one's empty!"

"I know."

"But... if you knew that, why didn't you refill it?"

Shrug. "You asked me to check them, not fill them."

The girl was simply infuriating.

"So, can anyone suggest any practical examples of how you could put any of these ideas into practice in your own store?" Trevor asked.

Shirley was stirred from her reverie by a flurry of hands shooting up into the air around her and she blinked and hastily focussed on the slide of bullets points behind Trevor.

Team Building Activities should:

- *Involve everyone*
- *Occur outside the working environment*
- *Generate camaraderie*

- *Foster co-operation*
- *Allow freedom of expression*
- *Provide opportunities for staff to take initiative*
- *Focus on fun where possible.*
- *Have a clear, common goal that everyone can contribute towards*
- *Generate a sense of shared achievement.*

"Yes, Su." Trevor nodded his head upwards towards Su Wiseman, manageress of a large store in Galashiels. The others put their hands down with an audible groan.

"Last year I organised a team weekend at one of those outward bound places? Where you play paintball, climb obstacle courses, abseil, clay pigeon shoot. All that. Everyone really enjoyed it!" Su looked patronisingly around at the class, smiling sweetly. Shirley wanted to throttle her. Her own hand shot up.

"Yes, Doreen?"

"Shirley." She corrected, clearing her throat, annoyed that Trevor knew Su's name and not hers. A small but rankling indicator of the aperture settings in the Greggs management camera. Su was clearly in the foreground, sharply in focus, while she was somewhere in the middle distance, an indistinct smudge off behind the main subject. "Does the company provide any funding towards these sort of team-building exercises?"

Trevor smiled, jagged yellow teeth showing dimly between his pale lips and veined cheeks. "Naturally. It is company policy to invest in its staff and, by your very presence here today, you can see, for example, our commitment to staff training."

Shirley smelled an evasion.

"How much?"

"Well now, that depends." Trevor's smile faded a smidge.

"On what?"

"Subsidies for team-building activities are available-"

"Subsidies?" Subsidy meant partial payment towards the cost, not full payment. She felt her ambitions for a successful outcome from this week falter, like a wartime pilot flying over enemy territory, low on fuel as the engines sputtered.

"Subsidies." Trevor continued, trying to stay smooth, but his smile had definitely slipped into something more like a grimace. "The values of which depend on individual branch profitability."

Shirley's hopes rose as the fuel gauge responded slightly to her tapping. Since Alasdair's arrival, takings had risen - there was still hope she could make it back across the Channel.

Big Paul flung open the heavy church door and gaped open-mouthed at the sight in front of him. The place was rocking and he stood, stunned as this wall of vitality and life hit him full in his broad chest.

Led by the black vicar and a couple of backing singers, large ladies draped in cloth of an ebullient colour and pattern like some kind of dazzle camouflage which confused the eye and foxed the senses, the microphones seemed totally unnecessary as their voices rang out and filled the space above his head, reverberating out into the bright chill behind him.

The entire congregation was standing, singing lustily and freely, unencumbered by social embarrassment or self-consciousness. What a contrast to the cold, sharp silence of a Scottish church that he recalled. He had never been a big churchgoer himself, but on those occasions where he had attended it had always been the same: a shuffling and mournful congregation sheepishly murmuring some obscure litany, hoping their individual voices wouldn't stand out too much amongst the crowd, each one grateful that the minister at the altar was leading them by lifting his own voice into prominence.

Here it seemed like a competition - last one to go unheard clears away after. The air in this bright, sunlit hall, all polished wood and burnished gold leaf, was vibrating with sheer energy. Everyone was swaying and clapping, bodies swinging to some ethereal rhythm they all seemed to possess - or that seemed to possess them. Was this what people meant when they talked about the Holy Spirit - some unseen life-force that infiltrated and possessed you so that you lost all sense of who and where you were?

How very un-Scottish.

There she stood, Paul could see, at the far end of the dais, front row, cheeks bursting with happiness and curls bouncing loose from her turban headdress as she glowed and sang and clapped along.

He let the door swing shut on its cushioned closure and stepped gently forward, taking up a position on the back row of seats - all of which were empty, as were the next eight or nine rows. All of the worshippers were pressed to the front as if to better absorb the energy and expressed truth emanating from the vicar and his disciples. No-one noticed him and Paul was glad of it. Here he could watch her with impunity and, while he was about it, work out how the hell he was supposed to approach her.

He didn't even know her name! He couldn't remember when he'd last been on a date, let alone asked for one.

How had he met Shirley? Buggered if he could remember. And anyway, whatever lines he'd used that'd worked on her probably wouldn't work here. This woman was not like Shirley, with this exuberant backdrop and all this fervour. If he did manage to ask her out, what would they talk about? What would they have in common? Even if it was just for show, he couldn't sit there in silence, could he? Maybe they could talk about religion.

But Paul didn't do religion, never had. His mother had made him attend Sunday school as a child but he had never got to grips with the basic premise of how one bloke dying took away everyone's sins. He'd asked for an explanation and not been given one, so found it much easier to stop attending and do his own bit of sinning instead. When his mother had found out she had been furious with him and stopped his pocket money for a week; his father had smirked and given him a quid when she wasn't looking.

When the song had ended - it seemed unfair to call it a hymn, such a mincing and unimpressive word - everyone sat and Paul did too, watching and listening intently as the vicar strode about the small stage incanting quotes and aphorisms with charismatic ease whilst his congregation lapped it up and punctuated his entreaties with "*Hallelujahs*" and "*Praise Thee Lods*". It was like watching a game show where the audience had been prepped to a fever pitch and were all excited to play their part, regardless of what this man said.

The preacher's eyes shone, brilliant white and chestnut brown, flashing along with his teeth as he opened his mouth wide, speaking in an off-kilter cadence, like he was deliberately picking the wrong syllables to emphasise and rushing through the others to get to them before anyone noticed

"We are righteous in the eyes of Thee Lod."

"Hallelujah!"

"And blessed, for we shall be saved. Who shall save us?"

"Thee Lod."

"And who is righteous?"

"His children."

"And who are his children?"

"We are! Praise thee Lod."

"And we, his children, shall glorify His name. The name of Thee Lod."

"Hallelujah!"

"For at Easter *time* we celebrate the cruci-*fix*-shone."

"Hallelujah!"

"And the resur-*rect*-shone."

"Praise Thee Lod!"

"Thee *Lod* who gave his only son, Jeez *U*, to take *a-way* thee sins of the *wold*."

"Hallelujah!"

"And we shall glorify His name by building thee true cross!"

"Praise thee Lod!"

"Thee true cross, here in this town, for this congre-*gay*-shone."

"Hallelujah!"

"And we will raise our *eyes* to thee *Lod* and sing His *pray*-ses at the foot of thee true *cross*."

"Praise thee Lod!"

"Praise thee Lod, indeed. Amen, my children."

"Amen."

At the end of this call-and-response, she rose and started walking, smiling, along the front row with a red plastic bucket. She paused at each chair as hands pulled purses and wallets from handbags and pockets. Paul could hear the sound of coins hitting the bottom and the jingling and chinking as she jiggled the bucket moving along the rows and a small fear niggled through him. Left to right and then right to left, slowly she snaked her way through the seats.

As she left each row behind her, the congregation rose and started filing out, chatter and laughter filling the air as coats were shucked on, hats planted on heads. Reaching the last occupied line, she looked up and saw him sitting there alone, many rows back from everyone else.

He smiled at her, sheepishly, and she returned an enormous grin and tottered towards him, this wooden cathedral gradually quietening as it emptied. By the time she reached him, Paul was aware of only of the two of them - and the fuzzy shape of the vicar in the distance, collecting hymn books and papers from the seats. She shook her bucket at him, the coins and notes rustling and ker-thunking in the echoey plastic. His eyes widened as he looked down and then back at her, blinking, as she innocently waited, one hand now on her hip.

"Erm... bit short I'm afraid. At the moment."

She cocked her head to one side and pursed her lips. A bower bird unsure how to deal with this strange intruder to her nest.

"Temporarily like." Paul added.

"You are new here, yes?"

"Aye." Was all he could manage. He blew out both cheeks. "I'm Paul."

"Paul." She said, as if it was the first time she'd ever heard that particular syllable. Then she threw him completely by asking him a question: "On thee road to

Damascus?"

"What?"

"Blessing!" The vicar called from behind her. "Is everything alright?"

Paul thought for a moment that he was back in the call-and-respond section of the show and then it dawned on him: *Blessing is her name!* Of course it was.

The vicar appeared over her shoulder, his face showing concern but the enormous smile still present.

"This is Paul." Blessing said. "A newcomer to our church."

"Paul! A newcomer! On thee road to Damascus! Praise thee Lod!" The vicar beamed at him and began pumping his hand like someone plunging a sink, one hand grasping Paul's own, the other wrapped on top of it as if he feared it would escape. "Welcome, welcome! As generous as your namesake?"

Paul didn't know who his namesake was nor who the question was directed at, but Blessing stepped in to vanquish his awkwardness. Only to then worsen it with her response.

"No, Isaiah." She said, her head down as if she was the one at fault. "Not today."

The vicar looked disconsolately down into the bucket and then raised his face back up to meet Paul's, the smile still present but its wattage somewhat dimmed. "You do not wish to make a donation to our Easter cele-*bray*-shone?"

"Oh, aye. I'll make a donation, right enough." Paul mumbled. "Haven't got any on me right now, mind."

Isaiah, still holding Paul's enormous hand, pulled it up between them, as if they were physically joined in prayer. "So why did thee Lod bring you to us today?"

Paul's brain told him to eschew the obvious, correct, answer. He shrugged. "Because he moves in a mysterious way?"

"He does move in mysterious ways, Paul." Isaiah nodded, eyes on fire. "Only thee Lod knows why he does things. But He always has a plan. Always a reason."

"Whatever you say, vicar." Paul said, wishing this man would let go of his hand.

"Please, I am not a vicar." Isaiah's teeth gleamed as he obligingly relinquished Paul's hand and spread his own arms wide. "This is not a church."

"Looks like a church." Paul blurted, regretting it immediately as the vicar grasped his hand again with renewed vigour.

"My friend, this is more than a church. It is a Ministry. Thee Global Light Revival Ministry for Renewed Christian Fellowship. A Ministry with many branches. This is but one." He beamed at Paul, enormous eyes drilling into him as if demanding a response.

"It's... lovely. Your Ministry."

"It is not *my* Ministry." Isaiah laughed, tightening his grip on Paul's hand. "It is thee Lod's Ministry. I am merely its servant. A humble servant of thee Lod."

"Right." Paul stood awkwardly, waiting.

The vicar put his hands down and then examined Paul's enormous mitt between his own black, slender fingers, tracing the palm and the lines upon it. "You have the hands of a labourer. The hands of someone used to heavy toil."

Paul avoided the urge to refute this claim. Isaiah lifted Paul's chin and looked deep into his eyes, then he stroked Paul's beard and traced the line of his nose. Unused to such intimate physical contact, Paul glanced nervously at

Blessing but she was smiling at him, indulging her vicar.

"You are a carpenter!" Proclaimed Isaiah. "A carpenter just like thee Lod Jeez U!"

Paul, dumbfounded, could barely nod.

"Thee Lod has brought you here to us! To help us! In His Mercy he has given you to us!"

Blessing started applauding in delight and Isaiah let go of Paul and raised his arms in the air.

"Praise Thee Lod! For He is all-knowing and all-seeing."

"Praise Thee Lod!" Rejoined Blessing.

"He has brought you here to build our cross! Hallelujah!"

"A what now?" Paul was stunned.

"A cross." Isaiah crowed.

"On a chain like?"

"No!" A massive grin reappeared. "Life-size."

"What?"

"Life-size. The size of the cross on which our Lod Jeez U was crucified." Isaiah's eyes sparkled and shone.

"Amen." Blessing intoned, lowering her face.

"It is to *be* the centre *piece*."

"Of what?"

"Our Easter cele-*bray*-shone. To glorify *His* name. The name of thee *Lod*."

"Right."

"At Easter *time* we celebrate the cruci-*fix*-shone and the resur-*rect*-shone. Thee *Lod* giving his only son, Jeez U, to take *away* thee sins of thee *wold*."

"Yeah. I heard that earlier."

"This is something you can make, yes?"

Paul looked at Blessing's eager face and then considered. "Depends how big you mean by *life size*."

"This is to *be* the centre *piece.*" Isaiah repeated. "A giant *cross* for my congre-*gay*-shone."

"Aye. But how giant?"

"Size is no obj-*ect.*"

"It is for me." Paul said. "I'm a sole trader." *Not a construction crew* he added, silently.

"Well then, as large as you can *make* it. I i-*mag*-ine you can *make* one to *glorify* thee *Lod?*"

"Happen." Paul nodded. "And, um, money, is that an object?"

"It shall be your contri-*bew*-shone to our Easter cele-*bray*-shone!"

Paul was aghast, but the devoted look he got from Blessing was some compensation. "Aye. But materials, like."

"Thee Lod will provide." Isaiah said, enigmatically, and Blessing rattled her bucket.

Paul wasn't up for enigmatic right now. "Up front?"

"Thee Lod asks that we all have faith." Isaiah spread his hands as if the words he spoke were nothing at all to do with him. "Trust in Him and you will be fully repaid."

"Cash?"

Isaiah grinned and pumped Paul's hand again. "God willing."

FOUR

"Okay. You win." Paul was shaking his massive head, an enormous grin plastered across it.

"Win what?" Cullen was back, wearing the most preposterous headgear Paul had ever seen. On him anyway. It made him look like a stock photo of a homeless alcoholic.

"The Oscar for Costume Design goes to..."

"Don't know what you're on about."

"The hat, man. What was the thinking? I'm supposing there was some thinking?"

"I thought I was cold so I thought I should get a hat."

"Wow. Well, as hats go it is..."

"What?"

"Spectacular." Paul brandished the word as if he had just coined it. "You know you're supposed to take the price tag off?"

"Glad you like it."

"I don't."

"And I'm not glad."

"Right, well, pleasantries concluded. What's brought you back here again so soon? I mean, don't get me wrong, always pleased to see you. I guess. It's just-"

"What?"

"Well, don't see you for months and then, voila, you're all over me like stink on sprouts."

Cullen was mute.

"Cat got your tongue?" Paul prodded.

"No. Didn't realise it was a question."

Paul sighed. "It wasn't. So, is that it then? I have to play Twenty Questions to wangle anything out of you? Alright then. Question One: Are you alive?"

Cullen regarded him deadpan.

"I'll take that as a Yes. Question Two: What've you been up to since I saw you last? Apart from buying a hat."

"Research."

"Huh. Should I punish you for not sticking to Yes and No answers, or should I be grateful you are willing to converse using actual words?"

"Grateful."

"If monosyllabically."

"I'm here to... what do they say... bounce something off you?"

"Fuck me." Paul's eyebrows shot up in alarm. "Is it a hammer?"

"Alas, No."

"Well...um, good." Although the expression on Paul's face said *doubtful.*

"You are always on at me about sharing. Information. It's good to share. *Et cetera.*"

Paul marvelled at the novelty of something he had said actually penetrating Cullen's skull. "Blimey! You're a dark wossname aren't you?"

"It has been remarked upon."

"Well, bounce away! I'm not one to look a dark horse in the mouth."

"Gift horse."

"I know! It was a wossname, Mister Chairman of the Pedantic Society."

"Actually, it's the Pedantry Society."

Paul sucked a tooth. Dealing with Cullen was often like trying to repot a cactus. "I'm not sure I'm gonna like this bouncing lark if this is anything to go by."

"I haven't started yet."

"Well, for God's sake get on with it."

"Right." Cullen took an unaccustomed breath. "Right."

"Come on! It's sharing, not Strictly. *Se-ven!*"

"What?"

"Never mind." Paul waved away his friend's confusion. "Begin."

"Okay. The proprietor of Bryce's is a Jehovah's Witness."

Paul waited but that seemed to be the end of Cullen's sentence. "Is this code?"

"No."

"Like: *the winter geese fly tonight?* Do I need a special phrase book or something?"

"No. It is exactly what it says. The proprietor of Bryce's-"

"Charles."

"Is that his name?"

"Aye. So please stop calling him *the proprietor of Bryce's*. Its like saying the *bell of my auntie's bicycle*. Wherever you're going with this, we'll get there quicker."

"Okay. Charles Bryce wears a lapel badge in the shape of the globe adorned with a banner which reads: JW.ORG."

"JW standing for Jehovah's Witness?"

"Correct."

Paul nodded and then stopped. "And?"

"Don't you see?"

"Sorry, is this a visual thing?"

"No."

"Then No, I don't see."

"What do you know about Jehovah's Witnesses?"

"They believe in God?"

"Yes." Cullen said, his brow furrowing.

"They go round knocking on doors trying to... dunno, convert you?"

"Yes. They do. Well, they did. Since it was Jesus's method of gaining disciples and they believe in following him, like for like."

"Doesn't work."

"No, that's why I said *did*."

"Oh. What do they do now, then?"

"They realised it wasn't working and moved with the times."

"So they're online?"

"No. They stand at certain junctions, in public - town squares, market crosses, that kind of thing - and display leaflets hoping people will show an interest."

"Moved with the times! What times - the Victorian?" Paul screwed up his features. "I wonder if that's why old Charlie boy got into that tussle with the reverend?"

"What?"

"Um, never mind."

Cullen blew out a sigh. "What else - do you know about them?"

"Pretty much it, really. I mean, I reckon they're all weird, with a pole up their arse and, like most religions, a hotbed of sexual frustration and/or kiddy fiddling but-"

"Let me stop you there. You reckon all that?"

"Oh aye."

"But you don't *know* any of it."

"Nah. But, see, you don't need to *know* stuff. Not when

you can *reckon* it. It's wossname isn't it? Inference?"

"Is it?"

"Aye."

"Not prejudice?"

"No!"

"Or bigotry?"

"You interested in what I reckon or not?"

"Well, sad as it is to admit it, in this instance I am going to have to say *yes* because you have hit some pretty big nails on the head there."

"Wow. Cool!" Paul preened.

"Let's come back to that. Meantime, here's the key phrase..." Cullen took a deep breath and exhaled very slowly and loudly. "*Ministerial Servant.*"

"You what?"

"Ministerial Servant?" Cullen repeated, looking at Paul intently. There was no sign of a reaction to the phrase.

"Is this code again?"

"No." Cullen's voice was cold and stern. "Are you saying that you are not familiar-"

"With the term Ministerial Servant? Correctamundo. Tumbleweed."

"Baxter's last words?"

Paul frowned, his brain scratching an itch of memory. "Baxter the egg farm bloke?"

"Yes."

"Who's dead?"

"Yes."

"Didn't know that."

"How could you not know that?"

"Was it in the papers?"

"I imagine so."

"Don't read the papers."

Cullen was exasperated. "I told you about it!"

"Why would you tell me about it?"

"I did tell you about it. I remember." Cullen shook his head, sadly. "I also remember that you were well into the Guinness in the sunshine when I told you."

Paul footled around for a memory that may or may not have been there. It was all the same to him.

"Tell me again."

"No." Cullen pursed his lips. "Here's the edited highlights: I have a daughter. She went missing a long time ago. I am trying to find her. A man called McKenna had something to do with it. I think Baxter knew McKenna. When I asked him-"

"Asked?"

"Pressed... him for information, all he gave me was *Ministerial Servant.*"

"Right!" Paul's eyes lit up and then, almost as suddenly, faded. "Which means...?"

Cullen sighed. "Ministerial Servant is a title that is bestowed on some people within the-"

"Jehovah's Witnesses" They finished together.

The pair sat in silence for a while: Cullen lost in his endless quest, forever circling key information without ever managing to quite grasp it - like a bird of prey with bad eyesight; Paul scanning back through this conversation they'd just had, marvelling at the amount he'd learnt about Cullen in so brief a time, and the many questions it left him with.

"So... this daughter?"

"He was in again, looking for you. While you were on your jolly." Traci was shaping a nail with an emery board while waiting for the green light on the coffee machine to come on.

"It was not a jolly. It was a management training course." Shirley was wiping down the work surfaces on her first day back, trying desperately to recall some of the *difficult staff role play* sessions she had taken part in.

"Same difference."

"Traci, please don't do that here. This is food preparation area. I have told you this many times before."

"S'only my nails! It's working here that snags 'em."

"I can only apologise for asking you to put effort in which might inflict damage to your cuticles." Shirley smiled, tightly.

"Come again?"

"Never mind. Did he say anything?" Shirley tried to act nonchalant but felt her heart pitter-patter at this news of persistence from Paul; persistence was not his strongest suit.

"Dunno. I didn't speak to him. *He* did." She threw her head back, blonde highlights revealing black roots, to indicate who the second *he* was, but Shirley knew. "And you never tell *him* off. He's always combing his hair over the cream cakes."

"Is he?"

"Always." Traci nodded in emphasis.

"Then I will have a word with him."

"Good." This seemed to satisfy Traci who stopped buffing and put the emery board in the pocket of her tabard.

Shirley pondered this news about Paul seeking her out while she filled the water reservoir. She hadn't seen him for ages - weeks now. She wondered-

"And another thing..." Traci piped up, disturbing

Shirley's musings. "The other day he was fiddling with his... you know... in his pants. Getting one thing straight, he called it. Right in front of Mrs McKay while she was waiting for her egg custard. No gloves nor nothing. It was disgusting."

"I wasn't aware-"

"You're always having a go at me but Mister Acting Manager? Oh no."

"Traci-"

"It's Alasdair this and Alasdair that and Alasdair the other. I don't get a look-in. All I get is abuse."

"I would hardly call it-"

"It's not fair!" Traci pouted. "I'm a long-standing employee. He's only been here five minutes. If there's perks or plum-jobs come up I should get first dibs."

"Who said there were any-"

"The other day. Tuesday it were. Or Thursday? When's half-day closing? Anyway, I was wiping down the thing, you know by the microwave, and he comes over, sneaking up like. All shiny like he does, you know? And he poked me! A real jab, both hands, in my kidneys. I almost banged my head on the extractor!"

"Really?"

"Said it were a joke, like. Just friendly messin' about between colleagues."

"Well, I-"

"Abuse is what I call it."

"Well, now I don't-"

"You should sack him!"

"I'll get right on it." Shirley drawled, thinking she'd rather slam her tits in a car door. Or Traci's.

Traci put her hands on her hips. "I should report him to a tribunal."

"What tribunal?"

"I don't know." Traci puffed. "That's your job, innit? HR. You're the one just been on a course. He shouldn't be allowed to do that."

Shirley sighed heavily. "I've said I'll have a word with him, and I will."

"About this as well?"

"About both things. All things." Shirley pursed her lips and crossed her arms. "Listen Traci. I realised that hiring Alasdair has..." *Put your nose out of joint? Disrupted the hierarchy? Thrown your low productivity levels into sharp relief?* "Meant changes, for us both. And I was wondering if perhaps it would be a good idea for us all to go out together, after work, one night. Go for a drink maybe, get to know each other better?"

Traci raised one eyebrow. "I don't want to be playing gooseberry!"

"Whatever do you mean?"

"Nothing. Just sayin'"

Shirley gave Traci a withering look. "Just saying what?"

"Nothing."

"Well, then. What about it? Do you think it's a good idea?"

"Just going for a drink?"

"Yes."

"The three of us?"

"Yes. Like a work's night out."

"With him?"

"Yes, all of us. A work's night out."

Traci considered this for a moment and, by the look on her face, it wasn't a pleasant mental image she was conjuring up. Shirley's mind raced, trying to sweeten the pot quickly before the idea was trampled underfoot.

"I'll be paying, of course."

"Will you?" Traci's eyes lit up.

"Yes." Shirley nodded, her enthusiasm suddenly tempered by an awareness that she had no idea of Traci's alcohol consumption or, indeed, preferences. Was she one of those women who only drank Jaegerbombs or Screaming Orgasms?

"Okay, then. When?"

"Well, I'll have to check with Alasdair but I thought Thursday - we could go to the Pub Quiz at the Lamb & Flag."

"This Thursday?"

"Yes. Are you doing anything?"

"No. Thursday's good." Traci looked up to the ceiling, perhaps mentally contemplating her wardrobe choices. Shirley could suddenly picture Traci in some scandalously scanty peel-off dress and glass heels revealing yards of orange flesh bearing multiple tattoos.

Oh well, thought Shirley. Now let's hope Alasdair is willing. We'll be a team. Have a common goal. We'll be communicating and discussing ideas. Having fun! The bullet points from her management training course swam in her vision. Wow. This might just work.

And, of course, Paul would be there.

Blessing looked down at the huge cross being constructed out on Paul's deck, watching this gigantic carpenter busy at work. Jesu's cross had, in all likelihood, been a crude and rudely constructed affair like this. Made from dark, unfinished wood it had been jagged, rough, uncomfortable and a final indignity for Our Lord - the equivalent of being buried alive in a pauper's grave. This facsimile before her seemed to match that original in every regard. She marvelled at this stunning attention to such exquisite detail - researched and thorough, the intention for verisimilitude palpable in every badly-chiselled mark, every poorly-planed stroke. This crude replica would indeed be a fitting tribute to the celebration for Lord Jesu.

Completely indifferent to her musings and attention, Paul worked away on autopilot. Unknown to Blessing, a focus on quality wasn't what you would remember Paul for, as anyone who knew him would tell you. Reliability, timekeeping, quality - these were the top three things on a very long list of things Paul was an easy stranger to. His heart was in the right place but somehow his standards never were. If he had ever sworn an occupational oath it would not have been one endorsed by Hippocrates, more likely Mediocrates. His attention to detail could be boiled down to a single word: *meh.*

"It is truly amazing." Blessing could not help articulate her thoughts, clasping both hands to her bosom almost in prayer. "You are a very good man, Paul."

Paul surprised himself by feeling a little tremble of delight when she said his name. He thought he might be blushing so kept his head down while he worked. "Call me Beep."

"Beep?"

"Yeah. Short for BP which is short for Big Paul. My mates call me Beep."

"Beep." Blessing tried out the sound of it. "Beep. Yes, I will. It is a nice name."

"Cheers."

"I am your friend, then?"

Her question brought Paul up short. He lurched to his feet but, feeling a twinge, stopped halfway. He realised it looked like he was on one knee but he couldn't help that right now. "Yeah, about that. See I wanted to ask you on a date, like? That's why I came to church."

Blessing sighed. "I do not have dates. I do Thee Lod's Wok."

"Oh. Right."

"But I can be your friend!"

Paul considered this for a moment. "Are you free Thursday?"

"For a date?"

"For a Pub Quiz."

"What is a Pub Queez." The words didn't sound quite right coming from her mouth - they sounded bright and sparkling, as if she had invented some new wondrous concept.

"It's a quiz. In a pub." Paul said, failing to clarify. "Like we're in a team and we have to answer questions. Best team wins."

"Will I be on your team?"

"'Course. Friends, innit?" Paul was delighted. It would look like he had a date, but it wouldn't be a date. And it would be the Pub Quiz, so they'd be sat answering questions in a group - he wouldn't have to make awkward conversation! Sometimes Paul impressed even himself.

"Yes, friends."

Blessing smiled, a broad gleam of a smile which illuminated her face and much of the day.

Blessing had no friends. Every day and every night she was called upon to do *Thee Lod's Wok*: part prayer, for being rescued from death; part calling, ministering to Isaiah as he carried *Thee Wod Of Thee Lod* out from Africa into the hearts of the people of Scotland.

Isaiah was her guardian and had been since she was

sixteen. Five years ago she and her father, Pious (proprietor of *Glory To Almighty God Sanitary & Waste Management Services Limited)* and twelve others, one of whom turned out to be Isaiah, were crammed into a *tro-tro,* a Ghanaian public transport workhorse which was a cross between a VW campervan and a demolition derby burnout. Halfway to Accra doing sixty on an unmade road, the tro-tro had blown a tyre, rolled over and ended up in a ditch. Her father and three others had died in the crash. Blessing had been thrown clear but broken both ankles. Isaiah had walked away from the crash, miraculously unscathed.

Isaiah with his dog collar and charisma (and lots of cash secreted into the palms of willing medical staff) had marshalled the accident scene and ensured she received the best care and surgical treatment possible. Her bones had knitted together well, her wounds had healed and, with His grace, she was soon walking and moving as well as she ever had.

His survival without a scratch, and her magical recovery, were gifts from The Divine And Heavenly Anointed Lord Jesu, Isaiah had proclaimed (conveniently overlooking the four poor souls who had perished in the crash, including her father). He took her under his wing and she came to live with him and his wife in their palatial ministerial residence on the outskirts of the capital, Accra.

After his wife died in mysterious circumstances, Isaiah decided to leave Ghana and build his Ministry out in the world. She had never understood why he had chosen Scotland but here they were. But new to the country and the climate, Blessing knew no-one other than Isaiah, and he gave her little time to herself. Isaiah with his outrageous smile, his exuberant energy, his vision and enormous dreams - he was simply too other, too huge, too engaged with fulfilling his mission and building his Ministry, to stop and think how she felt, what she might need. Isaiah was perpetually occupied and she was kept perpetually busy.

But Paul, on his road to Damascus, building a cross for her pastor! Surely Isaiah would not frown on a friendship with him? She looked up at Paul, then at the cross, then up at the sky.

"I shall be in your team and thee Lod shall help us win."

"Aye." Paul stroked his chin. "Well, he does work miracles doesn't he. Are you, um, any good at quizzes then?"

"I do not know." She looked at him with wide, hopeful eyes. "But you have made a fitting tribute for Lod Jeez U. It shall be a marvellous cele-*bray*-shone. He shall reward us."

"Cool."

She screwed up her face. "I shall need a new dress."

Paul's eyes widened in alarm. "For the Quiz?"

"For thee cele-*bray*-shone!" She laughed at him, a little girl again, and Paul felt momentarily young. She hooked her arm into his and tried, unsuccessfully, to pull him to his feet. "But I can wear it to thee quiz also. You will help me choose one?"

"You sure?" Paul asked. "I'm not known for my dress sense."

"Thee dress is for me, silly!"

"Yeah, I know." Paul winced, finally straightening up with an audible cracking sound and nursing his lower back with one hand. "No idea how we're going to get this down into town, mind. I can't carry it."

Blessing looked down at the cross, puzzled. "Thee Lod,

He carried it."

Paul sniffed. "He was younger than me. I'm nearly fifty you know. Young man's game this, carrying crosses."

"Thee Romans crucified women as well. All carried crosses for their sins."

"They didn't have my back. Plus, I don't have his genes do I?" Paul's reasoning was following its own track, doggedly persisting until it hit a buffer or ran out of rail.

"Genes?"

"Son of God, innit? I mean, who has?"

"We shall get thee cross down to thee town." Blessing said, simply. "Thee Lod will provide."

A thought occurred to Paul, and he marvelled at it for a moment.

"This *Lod will provide* malarkey. It's a bit like the soup, innit?"

"Thee soup?"

"Yeah. In fact, if you substitute the word *Soup* for *Lord*, I think we're saying the same thing."

"Thee soup will provide?" Blessing tried it out loud, disbelief registering on her pretty features. "What is this soup?"

"Let's just say it's my version of your Lord. For now. We can come back to that." Paul considered for a moment. "Anyway, whatever it is, Soup or Lord, it'll have to provide something pretty wonderful. Must be almost a mile into town. How far did He have to carry it?"

"Lord Jesu? It is said that he stumbled three times along thee Via Dolorosa - thee Way Of Suffering."

"Not surprised. It's a beast, that thing." Paul surveyed his handiwork. Made of old oak railway sleepers, jointed together, it measured some eighteen feet in height. He had creosoted the wood to darken it but oak didn't take kindly to treatment like that and refused to darken until it was good and ready. It already looked like it hadn't been treated at all but Blessing didn't seem to mind so he reckoned, on paper, it was all good.

"Couldn't we take it in pieces and construct it at thee site?"

"Blimey!" Paul wiped his brow with the back of a hand. "No-one said anything about making it in kit form. I've made these joints good and strong, screwed and glued them all together. Don't wanna damage it - maybe ruin it, now - by breaking it up."

"Maybe we could use a truck?"

Paul blinked, suddenly alarmed. "You can't use my van."

"You have a van?"

"Um." Paul grimaced, wishing he'd kept his mouth shut. "Yes. And No. Technically it is a van. For commercial purposes only with no personal benefit derived from it, whatsoever." Paul was always keen to stress this - one never knew if the taxman was listening. "But it is, sadly, no longer in showroom condition and about as liable to take the weight of this as my back. Plus, it would stick out. Dangerously. It's not a flatbed. Plus-"

Paul was feeling the need to press on with the case against using his van but Blessing was oblivious, focussed only on presenting Isaiah with a solution. "I can drive and you can walk behind it. Thee van can take thee weight of thee load and, driven slowly, you can walk behind it holding it safe and stopping it from falling out."

"Can you drive?"

"No. But you can show me?"

"Hmm. Insurance - that's a problem."

"You have insurance?"

"No, that's one of the problems. Besides, we'd still have to load it into my van. Which is parked up there." Paul thumbed indignantly up the slope behind his cabin to the loose track which acted as service road for all the cabins arranged along the valley sides. "Steep innit?"

"I shall bless you as long as you live if yee shall lift up thine hands in thee Lod's name, Jeez U said."

Paul was unimpressed. "Did I mention my back?"

FIVE

An enormous wooden cross was leaning against the Mercat Cross while a similarly huge man was heaving clods of soil out of the ground with a battered shovel.

Charles looked out from his shop window, aghast. Bad enough, defiling this ground. But with this cross! It was an outrage. He flew out of his shop and across the road.

"Excuse Me!" Charles puffed as he approached the giant workman.

"Ey up." The man glanced up from his labour and then turned his attention to the hole in the ground.

"I assume you have permission to dig this hole? From the council?"

"It's a hole." Said the man with a shrug. "It's not the Three Gorges."

"Irregardless." Charles bridled at the man's lack of concern. "Permission is required to disturb common ground or thoroughfares. Unless you have a license as, perhaps, a utility provider or similar?"

"No."

"Or maybe you are the owner of this patch of ground?"

"No."

"So may I enquire why you think you can just dig a hole here like this?"

"Just doing my wossname. Duty." The man leant on his shovel and nodded across to the church on North

Street. "Ask the Reverend over there. His idea. I'm just following orders. Maybe he's got permission?"

"Him!" Charles snorted. "Don't you worry, I very well intend to. In the meantime, until this is resolved, perhaps you could desist from digging?"

The huge workman puffed out both cheeks while he considered this suggestion for a moment, before deciding. "Alright."

"Good. And might I suggest that you do NOT attempt to inter this... this abomination AT ALL!" Charles blustered. "You do realise this is not the true cross?"

"Oh, I know that." The man scratched the side of his nose. "I made it."

"That is not what I meant. This..." Charles threw a hand towards the cross, scarcely able to bring himself to look at it. "This is not the cross that our Lord was crucified on."

"Just said that. I made it."

"This is not the right design." Charles spat through gritted teeth.

"Eh?" The man contemplated his workmanship, face screwed up. "What's wrong with it? Solid oak that, none of your chipboard or nothing."

"I said 'design', not materials." The man looked at him blankly so Charles thrust his neck forward and spoke slowly. "It's the wrong shape."

"It's a cross, mate. How can it be the wrong shape? It's cross-shaped. The shape of a cross. QED."

"My good man, that is what is known as a *crux immissa*. As opposed to, say, a *crux quadranta* or a *crux decussata*." Charles sneered, a sarcastic smile twisting his lips. "Notwithstanding that, our Lord was crucified on none of those. He was crucified on a *crux simplex*. This is not a *crux simplex* and therefore it is the wrong shape. QED."

"I dunno what you're on about, mate. It's a bloomin' cross, innit? Seen 'em in the bible, on TV and round people's necks. Look - there's one over there outside that church! A cross is a cross. This is a cross."

"The cross to which you refer, a *crux immissa* as I say, is wrong. All those crosses you see are wrong. It's a common mistake, I grant you, but a mistake nonetheless."

The giant exhaled sharply, clearly displeased. "Are you telling me I don't know what a cross is? That fella asks me to build one and I've built it wrong?"

"I'm not suggesting you have constructed this incorrectly." Charles raised both hands as a distancing gesture, suddenly worried at the dark look on this man's face. "Merely that perhaps the order you were given was wrong."

The man's eyes narrowed. "Go on then, pal. I'll bite. What should it look like, then?"

"Our Lord was crucified on a *crux simplex*. That is Latin for *a simple cross*."

"You can't get much more simple than this!" Sniffed the man, unimpressed.

"A *crux simplex* does not have a transom."

"A what?"

"A transom." Charles searched for a simpler word. "A cross-piece."

"How can it be a cross if it doesn't have a cross-piece?"

"Well, there I suppose you have me. I am not a linguist. Nevertheless, a *crux simplex* is referred to as a cross."

"So, you mean, just... a pole?"

"A simple stake, yes. Without a transom."

"Jesus was crucified up a pole?"

"Correct."

The man sighed and shook his head. "Well, on the one hand I think you're barking 'cos, like I said, everyone knows what a cross looks like. On the other hand, it woulda been a lot easier to build a cross wossname. In fact, building would be a bit of a misnomer wouldn't it? Coulda just got a telegraph pole and chopped it in half."

"Perhaps." Charles had no intention of disagreeing with the man further but his comments had clearly set a train of thought in motion that was not going to stop until it had run its course.

"And I had to buy this wood. And then there's the labour. If he's only going to pay me for a cross wossname when I've built a cross, er, cross... I'm not going to be happy."

"No. Quite." Charles started to step away from the man who now seemed to be getting quite agitated. "Why don't you, erm, leave this hole for now, hmm? Maybe go and check with your, erm, boss?"

"Damn right." The man flung the shovel to the ground and stomped off towards North Street. Charles watched him go and, the minute he was out of sight, he picked up the shovel and scurried back to his shop.

"She only wanted me to carry it! I mean, enough's enough."

Paul had been sitting on his deck, thoughtfully drinking from a can, when Cullen had appeared - unexpectedly again.

Cullen gave him an amused look. "Jesus had to."

"I know, right?"

"You could make it you very own Via Dolorosa."

"Don't you start!" Paul grunted. "I'm not doing any via

wossname. End of."

"You'd be doing the Lord's work."

"Are you winding me up?" Paul asked. "You're winding me up."

"You know - and I can't believe I'm about to say this-"

"Then don't."

Cullen paused, considered what he was about to say and then went ahead anyway, Paul's resentment notwithstanding. "You've got quite a lot in common with Jesus."

"Oh, fuck off!"

"No, really. Let's look at the evidence: you're both carpenters."

"Joiner."

"Same difference." Cullen said. "And, whilst I am no biblical scholar, I think it likely that neither of you spent a lot of time actually doing carpentry."

"Excuse me. That cross? Exhibit A."

Cullen ignored him, tolling off the points he was making on his fingers. "Both unmarried, neither of you had children."

"Yet."

"Both philosophers, in their own way."

"Ah, well. That's true."

"Both believe in a higher power."

"Eh?"

"Jesus and God; you and the soup."

"Oh aye." Paul probed a thoughtful tooth with his tongue. The soup was Paul's providence and saviour all rolled into one. The universe looking after him and providing him with solutions and answers without seeming to require him to so much as lift a finger. Which, for Paul, was incredibly handy. By failing to address a tricky situation through idleness or lack of creativity, he allowed sufficient time to pass after a problem revealed itself so that something unanticipated (aka *the soup*) interceded and removed the problem for him. It was like having his own guardian angel.

"I wonder..."

"Don't suppose your mother was a virgin?" Cullen teased, but Paul was lost contemplating something eternal. Cullen left him in silence until Paul's thoughts had run their course. Sitting on the deck in this spring morning was not an unpleasant way to pass the time. Ant and Dec, sharing his view, snoozed peacefully at their master's feet.

"Why do you think he was a carpenter?" Paul asked eventually.

"Not with you."

"Well, the Middle East? Not a lot of trees are there?" Paul mused. "He obviously didn't want the working with wood to get in the way of his preaching."

"I believe I made that very point just a moment ago."

"He should have been a brickie really, shouldn't he? All that mud. You could dry it in the sun for bricks. And all that sand for mortar. Or a plasterer. But not a chippie - doesn't make sense."

"Well, I'm glad you are attacking the credibility of Christianity where it matters, and not on some obtruse technicalities like what it says in the bible or any of its religious teachings."

"I'm not attacking Christianity. Just sayin' seems odd Jesus was a chippie - all things considered."

"Yes. Well, I'm sure theologians somewhere have pondered this profoundly and produced a substantial treatise on the subject. Somewhere."

Paul sighed, his ruminations at an end. "Anyway, where

was I? Oh yeah. Also, this Bryce bloke tells me it's the wrong sort of cross! I mean, what the actual?"

"That's a Jehovah's Witness thing."

"Aye. Well, not only was he very insistent he's also on some bloody town council or something. High up. Influence. Whatever. Bloody nutter. Anyway - detail, irrelevant. Point is: it'll have to go up after dark now, clandestine like, otherwise I'll never get it up."

"Tricky."

"You're telling me. Plus - can't put it up on my own. It's a two-man job and that pastor bloke's about as much use as a pastry powertool."

Cullen's eyes narrowed. "I feel that you might-"

"Correctamundo! It's a two-man job and we - you and me - are two men." Paul looked up to the sky. "Oh, Blessed be The Soup for bringing you to me!"

Charles gave a sharp intake of breath so loud that he involuntarily stepped back and bruised himself on the door handle behind him. He covered his mouth with one hand and froze. Had anyone heard him?

He blinked and looked again at the image currently running from Changing Room 3, transfixed. He'd just been standing before his desk checking the cameras for the day when the black woman with the exquisite feet had stepped into the picture and dropped her dress to the floor.

He moved forward and sat down at his desk, leaning close to the monitor. She was beautiful, exotic, gorgeous and completely alien. Charles shivered and the hairs on his arms and neck stood to attention.

She had her naked back towards him, a thin white bra

strap like a fresh weal across her shoulder blades. His eyes roamed all over her glistening, exposed skin. She was shucking a dress over her head and calling to someone, her appalling preacher friend maybe, on the other side of the changing room door. She let the dress slip down her arms and slink over her torso, bringing her elegant hands around to her back to find the zipper. Her fingernails were a delicate pink, like her toenails - the pink of a baby's mouth.

This ebony animal was a newly-formed creation, a fantastical beast unknown to him until now, which miraculously touched something deep inside him, flipped some switch which caused a torrent of desire to surge within him and rise up, a fountain of want and need coursing through him. Charles reached unthinkingly for his groin.

He had to get close to this woman in his shop - watching on a screen wasn't good enough now. He had to caress her feet, touch her velvet skin, sense her tropical warmth, inhale her perfume. He watched as one dress went off and another went on, then another. His eyes roamed across the moving image, his fingers stroking the screen. Surely she'd like some new shoes to go with her dress?

Charles exhaled slowly and thoughtfully. He stood up, straightened his clothing and headed down to the shoe department.

The last time Paul had spent longer than ten minutes in a clothes shop was when Shirley had asked him to help her pick out an outfit for the Melrose Sevens a few years back. It had started raining so he had agreed to enter until it stopped - and she'd also promised him a pork pie ploughman's for lunch afterwards. In the end she'd been unable to find anything she liked and he had argued that a new outfit wasn't required anyway. They'd gone along, dressed casually, only for Shirley to be embarrassed that *everyone else was dressed for Ascot and they were dressed for Farmfoods.*

And she'd never bought him that ploughman's.

Now here he was trying his hardest to smile and give Blessing the benefit of his sketchy opinion about female fashion. She didn't seem to care, however, judging by the enthusiasm and delight on her face with every new item she pulled off the rack.

He looked down at the clutch of fabric on his lap as he sat outside the changing room in Bryce's. This top one screamed of Debenham's perfume counter. Blessing emerged wearing an orange number with a chiffon scarf around her neck. She pirouetted proudly.

"Well?"

"All a bit Easyjet cabin crew, isn't it?" He blurted.

Blessing frowned. "Does that mean you like?"

Paul winced so she wordlessly grabbed the next dress from his lap and disappeared back behind the door.

Charles could trace his fascination with feet back to a flamboyant next-door neighbour he had as a child. A foreign woman, bleached blonde hair which showed black roots as if intentionally, thick makeup which made her eyes black and her lips red and polished nails which spangled like talons in the light. One summer, in those halcyon days when summers lasted forever and the sky was always blue, he had looked out of his bedroom window - where, perhaps, he had been indulging in shameful acts because he was alone, inside, hidden. Safe.

Out of his window he saw this beautiful creature emerge from her own kitchen in a bikini, bright and orange and like something from a French film, impossibly glamorous and, although he didn't realise it or even know the word at the time, sexy. She stepped out from the shade of her house into her small garden and lay on a rickety sun-lounger, a paperback shielding her eyes, wiggling with pleasure in the warmth of the afternoon as she tanned. And what a tan. Her body, olive-skinned to start with, glistened and gleamed with the lotion she had applied and her breasts heaved as she inhaled and exhaled slowly while she read.

And her toes. Charles couldn't recall ever having seen such things wondrous before. They were painted a marvellous, fantastic red. Pillar-box red. Telephone red. Lipstick red. As extraordinary a thing as he had ever seen, these toes seemed to bring her feet to life - promote them from a walk-on supporting role to the main feature. And, of course, there were ten of them - count them - ten gleaming, wiggling, outrageously decorated toes promising ten times the possibilities, ten times the pleasure. What that pleasure was or where it came from he could not possibly have said nor understood. Nor could he explain it.

He had seen toes before, of course he had! His own, those of his parents, those of the other kids in his class when they went swimming or played at the beach. But his mother didn't paint her toenails. Charles had never realised that this was actually a thing. Was it legal, he wondered? Did other women do this secretly and hide their shame inside their shoes? Was there a whole population of these furtive souls with perfect, desirable painted toes squirrelled away inside high heels - a potent combination which created an overpowering mental image in the head of that seven year-old. An image which seared itself on his retina and which, years later, he had subconsciously acquired the wherewithal and facilities to acquire and enjoy.

Over the succeeding few years he had taken every opportunity life presented to snatch a glimpse at naked female feet. Once, he recalled gloriously, some cousins had come to stay overnight and he had to share a bed with Natalie, them both being young and innocent - in a household short of beds this was perfectly normal.

Somehow he had plucked up the courage to invent a game in bed that Natalie had agreed to and he was able to squirrel himself down under the sheets while she stayed still and get his eyes and nose right up to her warm, smooth feet. He recalled getting breathless, partly due to the suffocating weight of the bedding above his head and the confined quarters he was sharing with Natalie's magnificent toes, but also because of his racing heart, some pulse of pleasure which had him blinking and gasping.

He could smell the fragrance now, her toes had smelled of nakedness and pinkness. And foolishly he had succumbed to touching them, unable to resist and stop at proximity and sight and smell. Natalie had jerked away, tickled, and started wriggling and giggling and Charles had urgently come up for air and lay perfectly still beside her, not touching her at all and listening intently for any sign that an adult under their roof had heard the results of this appalling act of indecency.

Natalie, who had been two years older than him, had

just smiled sweetly at him as if she had just won some hold over him and he was now in her easy and charming power. Neither child ever spoke of it again.

But for Charles, his taste for feet grew. Through adolescence he may have mused about calves and the way they curved up from slender ankles, strangely able to be simultaneously taut and supple, firm and soft. Or that beautiful dimple at the back of a knee, which vanished with each stride until reappearing again, winking at him. But feet was where it was at for him. Soon Charles was helping out after school in the family business - taking every chance he could to linger around the womens' shoe section at Bryce's.

And shoes, womens shoes, became a perfect holder for his lusts and desires. The objects themselves were sexy and when combined with a woman's toes, heel, and ankle - all of which he got to touch and caress, stroke and smell, as he removed the precious shoe from its tissue clad nook, an idol worthy of veneration which women lusted after like gold. You couldn't justify touching a woman's feet for a pair of wellies or espadrilles, but for nice, expensive heels the simple action of purchasing became more one of worship, a procession where the shoe was paraded, flaunted, honoured, venerated, before being acquired - more like buying a pet than a shoe.

Today's shoes, at least his stock, were often handmade with the delicate architecture of a spacecraft, the technology contained within them allowing paper-thin lines to support a woman's full weight on two heels smaller than a square centimetre combined. Like a gleaming suspension bridge which stretched out towards a far riverbank lost in the mist, the architecture was inspiring, elegant and immense - and the comparative costs were not too dissimilar either.

High-end shoes was where it was at and, for many women, Bryce's was a temple, a destination worthy of pilgrimage from many miles away because there was another beautiful thing about these shoes - you needed to touch them and be touched by them. Feel the harness on your feet, see the effect in the mirror, emotion was a huge element which transmuted a simple transaction into an act of worship.

When his father died, Charles became the high priest at this shrine to shoes and, as such, got to fondle and admire, coo and swoon, hiding his passion in plain sight while his customers couldn't see his lust for the dazzling glamour of the subject of their own quest.

But he eventually found he was recalling and treasuring the memory of each sole encounter more than the actual opportunity when it presented itself. Somehow the client interaction diluted his enjoyment, distracted him from focussing fully on the sensation, requiring him to be the agent and not observer at the moment of sale. What he needed was a way to capture the experience completely so that he could relive it again and again, in private, away from shame, no prying eyes or judgemental views to taint the experiences.

So his thoughts had turned to spy cameras and hidden CCTV. State of the art equipment researched, acquired and then painstakingly installed. He had purchased pull-down screens for his display window - to protect the stock from sun damage, he told customers - but which allowed him to work in the shop after hours, unseen, while he drilled holes and traced channels for hidden wires and cables to allow the, ahem, footage to be delivered to a network drive for later viewing.

And why stop at shoes? There were changing rooms in lingerie and ladieswear too. Be a shame to spend all this money on a superb network and leave a few nooks and crannies uncovered, wouldn't it? All those semi-naked women turning this way in that in front of a mirror wearing little more than a tantalising pair of heels and an innocent smile.

Charles Aloysius Bryce wasn't one to let an opportunity go to waste.

Eventually Blessing came out wearing a bright summer dress, short at the sleeves, emblazoned with huge colourful flowers. Even Paul had to admit that, with her colouring and figure, she looked fantastic.

"Knockout." He said, nodding. "Can we go now?"

Blessing beamed in gratitude, twirling again and admiring her reflection in the mirror.

"I hope I look smart for your friends."

Paul thought she wouldn't say that if she'd met his friends, but he kept his counsel.

"Beautiful. Quite, quite beautiful."

Charles marvelled at Blessing in her dress and clasped his hands together in praise at her ensemble. "You will want some lovely white sandals to go with that gorgeous outfit, perhaps? Something delicate and strappy to show off Madam's slender feet?"

"Oh yes! Sandals!" The woman clapped happily. "In Ghana, we wear sandals all the time."

"I think we're good." Argued a deep voice and Charles turned to find the giant who'd been trying to erect the wrong cross towering over him.

"Oh. It's you."

"Yes. It is."

Charles swallowed and performed a rapid mental assessment of the situation. On the one hand, here was this beautiful creature he just had to be near, who had agreed to try on some sandals - he'd get to touch her feet! On the other hand, here was her bruiser companion: a rude and unwelcome presence in his store who he would ordinarily eject and inform never to cross his threshold again.

Oh, it was no contest. Who was he kidding? He would suffer this giant a thousand times if it meant he had the chance to possess this woman's soles.

"I think, perhaps, Madam might really like our latest line of summer sandals. We have them in white." Charles ran his tongue over his teeth and gave his smoothest smile, which she returned and then skipped over to the shoe displays.

His heart thumping, Charles followed her, the giant forgotten. She had already pulled a strappy white sandal off the display and was sitting down. Charles rushed to her aid.

"Let me, Madam." He took the shoe from her and, trying to control his breathing, knelt beside her. He gathered up her perfect black heel in the palm of his hand, spooning the shoe beneath her foot as he did so. He inhaled deeply. She smelt of fresh soap and of hot sun on skin. His fingers trembled as he tried to close the strap across her ankle.

"I think Madam might need a smaller size." Struggling to steady himself as he stood, he swayed into the cool of the stockroom, shivering with anticipation at what he knew would be the most memorable moments of his life.

SIX

"Will you introduce me to your team mates?" Blessing asked, nervously tugging at her new dress, as they approached the pub.

"'Course." Paul shrugged.

"What will you say?"

"Eh?"

"How will you introduce me?"

"Um, friend?"

"Okay." Blessing, folded her gloved hands in front of her, seemingly satisfied with his answer. Paul held the door open for her and then felt time suddenly slow to a crawl. The hum and bustle that emanated from the doorway mingled with the warm, beery fug as the pair of them passed inside. In the time it took for Blessing to say "Are any of them here yet?" the air had turned chill and the Lamb & Flag had fallen silent. Paul appeared from behind Blessing's flamboyant outfit to find everyone in the pub staring at them.

"Wotcha." Paul grinned his usual grin and cast a practised eye over the familiar faces ranged in front of him. Seeing his grinning face, the locals exhaled as one and instantly the chatter resumed, in certain corners now more animated as many wide eyes followed Paul and his companion to the bar.

Paul surveyed the gloomy interior of the Lamb & Flag

with its drab wallpaper scattered with greying photographs of the town from the nineteenth century. The dark wood furniture marked and scuffed, cracked and old - and not in a good, antique patina added-value way; more in a mock-mahogany-from-Argos-hanging-on-for-dear-life way. Paul knew not to think of it as mahogany, partially through professional experience but mostly because he knew Davy the landlord held his purse strings with all the grip of a jockey's right hand.

"Alright, Beep." Davy stood behind the bar in his usual uniform of black trousers, black shirt and maroon waistcoat. Thin and gaunt, with wispy hair and a sallow complexion, he looked like a goth Uriah Heep. He pushed a pale green pint glass towards Paul whilst looking askance at Blessing.

"What's this?" Paul nodded down at the pint.

"Lime and Soda. The usual."

"Give over. Back on the old usual now, mate."

"Oh." Davy's face fell further towards the floor, now looking not just at reduced profit margin from the copious pints of soft drink that Paul could put away but at the fact that he'd have to throw this one away since none of his other regulars would touch the stuff. He moved to put it under the bar - you never knew.

"What is that?" Blessing asked, as he did so.

"This? Lime and Soda." Davy's eyes lit up. "Very refreshing."

"I will have that, please."

"And an IPA, Davy. Make that two."

Davy looked quizzically at Paul who merely shrugged and said: "Been shopping."

The landlord pulled two pints but looked at Blessing as he placed them down on the bar. "Here for the quiz then?"

"Yes." She replied, pleased with her initial taste of the Lime and Soda. She broke into her normal smile. "I am on Paul's team!"

"Ah well. Every little helps, eh Beep?"

"Yeah. Cheers."

Paul led Blessing through the pub, weaving through the tables as they went. He kept half an eye out for his team mates and half an eye for Shirley. He couldn't wait to see the look on her face when she saw him with Blessing. Paul spotted a booth on the far side of the pub, currently occupied by a burly, heavily tattooed man in a faded, too-tight, rugby shirt. He had a face like a slightly burnt brandy snap.

"Wotcha, Slash."

The man, busy perusing a menu, looked up casually at this familiar voice and then physically sat back in his seat.

"Fuck me!"

Paul glared silently at him, his eyes burning. The man with the menu swallowed hard, bit his lip and stayed silent.

"Blessing, this is Slasher. Specialist subject: Sport."

"Slasher?"

"Aye. Real name, Kenny, but everyone calls him Slasher."

"Why?"

"Because..." Kenny announced, proudly. "If you leave a drink on the table and turn your back on it..."

Paul's eyes stopped him in his tracks but Blessing stood waiting for him to finish.

"What? What will happen?"

"Doesn't matter, luv." Kenny snorted, looking at the pale green liquid in her glass. "Looks like someone's already had a go at yours."

Blessing tucked her dress underneath her and sat

gingerly down next to Paul who had already snuck in next to Kenny. She was still perplexed by the origin of the man's nickname.

Kenny reapplied himself to his reading material, shaking his head. Paul nodded, unseen, at the menu.

"It's new."

"I can fucking see that. What's going on? Where's the usuals?"

Beside him, Paul felt Blessing flinch.

"Davy's branching out." He said through gritted teeth.

"What for?" Kenny looked up, his face clouded with all the disappointment of someone who has just learnt of the term *lettuce wrap*. "It's like some bush tucker trial - loads of options that'll make you retch."

Paul just shrugged. "I think he's trying to capitalise on the temporary closure of the chippy." He leant in, confiding. "They've got mice."

"Fuck do I care? I don't go to the chippy to be healthy." Kenny flung the menu onto the table in despair. "If he's trying to capitalise on the closure of the chippy, where's the fucking chips? Jesus Christ."

Paul saw Blessing's hands tighten in her lap, her face down.

"He won't do chips." Said Paul, trying to calm Kenny. "Not proper chips, anyway. Says you need specialist kit which he don't have."

"Specialist kit? Davy thinks the smoke alarm's a fucking timer! Specialist kit."

"And he's worried that oven chips will compare... unfavourably."

"Unfavourably? I'll give him unfavourably. Fucking Davy." Kenny shook his head and the flesh in his neck quivered terribly. "Jesus Christ. What a bellend."

"Excuse me, Mr Slasher. May I interrupt you for a moment?"

Kenny looked stunned, glanced at Paul for some guidance as to how to converse with the exotic stranger and, none forthcoming, uttered a strangled. "Aye."

"I couldn't help noticing that you have just mentioned a very good friend of mine."

Kenny frowned. "Davy?"

"No, not Davy. Our Lord Jeez U. You took his name in vain."

"What?" Kenny was dumbfounded.

"Our Lord Jeez U. You took his name in vain. Twice." Blessing's eyes were moist and she bit her lip as she spoke.

He looked at Paul again who was now glaring at him intently.

"Er, sorry. Like. Um. I didn't mean to, um, you know-"

Paul reached for her hands but she folded them away out of reach. "Blessing. I'm sorry. Maybe it wasn't a good idea to bring you to the Quiz."

She shook her head, sadly, and sniffed. "Do you have a handkerchief?"

Paul exchanged a blank look with Kenny. "Maybe try the Ladies?"

She looked up at him, her big brown eyes wet with tears. He nodded behind him to indicate the location of the toilets. Blessing sniffed loudly, shuffled out of the booth and headed off in that direction, head down.

Paul watched her retreat and when she was out of earshot, turned back to Kenny.

"For fuck's sake, Slash-"

"What the fuck's going on here?" Kenny interrupted.

"She's a ... friend. Not from round here."

"I can fucking see that!" Kenny marvelled. "Y*ou've just mentioned a very good friend of mine: Jesus Christ!* First the menu, now this. Is everything changing now? Who agreed all this and why was I not informed?"

"Just... be nice. She's... delicate. Mind your language."

"Mind *my* language? You're the one just said *for fuck's sake*!"

Paul sighed. "For God's sake-"

"You cannae say that, either! She's a fucking God Botherer!"

"She's Ghanaian."

"A fucking African God Botherer!"

"Can you stop swearing?"

Kenny grumped. "I'll do ma best. Only when she's around, mind."

"Good enough." Paul relented.

Kenny shook his head. "It's a fucking mystery to me how you manage to pick up women."

"Lift from the knees. Look, she's just a friend."

"Oh aye." He moaned. "It's not fair. I may not be handsome. Or smart. Or athletic. Or gifted." With each statement his face fell.

"But?"

"Sorry, forgot where I was going with that. Where did you find her anyway, this... friend? Where do you go to meet women round here? There isn't anywhere."

"There's here!" Paul said, gesturing extravagantly around the pub.

"Good one."

"It wasn't here, anyway. It was church."

"Aw, Christ. Fucking God Botherer!"

"Keep your voice down." Paul hissed, looking around praying that Blessing wasn't back yet. "And stop saying

God Botherer."

The lights in Bryce's were still on but the store was closing. Large brown roller blinds, emblazoned with the Bryce's logo in blue, had been lowered over some of the ground floor windows and the front door. Cullen watched as another blind was lowered and he could see who was doing the lowering. He strode down the side of the building, along an alleyway to a door and window overlooking the bins. There were no blinds here and the door was unlocked.

Cullen crept inside and looked for somewhere to conceal himself. He would wait until dark. He was good at waiting. But was it going to be worth the wait? The chances that Bryce was the exact Ministerial Servant Baxter had referred to was possible - Baxter's farm was only a few miles up the road and the two men had obviously both been born into wealth and entitlement. But it was a long shot. A very long shot.

He reached into his pocket for the Polaroid before he remembered it was no longer there. The only photo he had left of his daughter, the one remaining record of her appearance, he'd had to surrender to the police for their records, potential evidence in their search for her. He closed his eyes and tried to picture Eilidh's face. Failing, he clenched his fists tight, his nails biting into his palms, the injustice burning hot through him.

No matter how unlikely the connection to Bryce, it was a lead - the only one he had. He owed it to her to follow it. Nothing else mattered to him anymore. Nothing.

From behind a curtain he suddenly heard women's voices, hushed and conspiratorial. Shaken from his thoughts, Cullen stepped over and listened.

"It was disgusting. Just disgusting. He was drooling, I swear to God, actually drooling. I had to send him away!"

"He makes my skin crawl, Joanne, he really does. The way he fawns over these women. It's so..."

"Obsequious?"

"Yes! And transparent? I mean, he's old enough to be their father, some of them."

"I don't think he cares, you know? I've seen him go weak at the knees, slavering at some old dear's ankles. Makes me want to retch."

"And he's got no sense of boundaries! He'll touch you, lean over you, stroke you, invade your personal space and leer at you! I mean, it's appalling."

"You should've seen this one today, though. She was black. Young and black and pretty. Oh my God, he couldn't have made it more obvious!"

"Well, I've had enough. I'm looking for another job. Don't care what is, I'll work a checkout if I have to. When I get home at night from here, I need a shower to clean myself off. Enough's enough."

"Someone should do something. If it wasn't for my Dennis I wouldn't be working here, I can tell you. Someone should definitely do something."

In the darkness, as the womens' voices receded, Cullen felt the hairs rise on his arms. Maybe it wasn't such a long shot after all.

"There we are ladies - one dry sherry, large..." Alasdair, dentures aglow in the reflections from the fire, daintily plucked the schooner from the tray and placed it on a beermat in front of Shirley. "And one Boys Are Stupid."

He almost threw this at Traci but she was already two drinks in and failing to notice much of the evening's proceedings.

"Thank you, Alasdair. It's very kind of you. But there's no need. I already explained that Greggs will foot the bill tonight." Shirley inhaled a heady, woody fragrance coming from Alasdair's open neck shirt and caught just a hint of auburn chest hair curling away behind the cotton.

"What is in that, Traci?" The drink in front of her looked more like a chocolate ice cream float than a cocktail.

"Baileys. Rum. Something." She sucked some up through a straw, hiccoughed and pulled a strange face. "'Sreally nice."

"That is exceedingly generous of the company. I'm a big fan." Alasdair fawned, removing his own glass of Scotch and its accompanying small jug of water from the tray. He placed the tray down by the side of his chair and hitched his chair closer to Shirley, a little further away from Traci. "So, how does this work again?"

"S'posed to be team building, innit?" Traci slurred. "There's no *I* in team, you know."

"I hope you're both good at general knowledge." Shirley tried to impart some enthusiasm to the table. "I'm afraid I'm probably not going to be much help. Got most of my Pub Quiz knowledge from P-" She stopped herself just in time but couldn't resist glancing over to a booth over on the far wall where she thought she had heard Paul's booming voice, but all she could see was the back of his head.

"I assure you, Shirley, a woman of your experience will have squirrelled away a lot of useful knowledge. Probably doesn't get stirred up under normal, behind-the-counter, conditions." He twinkled. "But I feel confident that, when push comes to shove, it'll pop to the surface when needed. So, what shall we call ourselves?"

He took control of the team pencil and paper and brandished it with a smile.

"Do you have any ideas?" Shirley prodded Traci, doing all she could to foster a team-building air.

"Of course not!" Alasdair snorted under his breath.

Traci, sucking hard on her blocked straw, came up for breath.

"What about *Boys Are Stupid?*"

"I don't think that's... appropriate. How about something related to Greggs? Can you think of something work-related that would work as a team name?"

Traci thought for a millisecond. "Short answer: no."

"I see. Long answer?"

"No-o-o-o-o-o-o."

"How about The French Fancies?" Offered Alasdair.

Shirley pondered. "Hmm. Well, none of us are French for a start."

"No, but some of us are fancy." He waggled his eyebrows.

"Doesn't quite say... successful team though, does it?"

"Or French Fondants?"

"Again, I'm not seeing how *French* works for us."

"It works for us more than she does." Alasdair muttered, jerking his head towards Traci. "And some of us are fond of others."

"And some of us are even fonder of ourselves." Snarked Traci.

Shirley stifled a rebuke - this team-building lark was harder than Trevor had made out. She gazed around her, trying to think of a name, while her two employees bickered between themselves.

"What about The Flaky Pastries?" Alasdair sneered.

"Butter Wouldn't Melt?" Traci retorted.

"Rolls for £1?"

"Sausage baguette - small?"

"Shirley, this is no good." Alasdair surrendered. "Can't you think of anything?"

"Hmm?" Shirley wasn't listening. She was dumbstruck. A slim, elegant black woman had just risen up next to Paul. She was wearing a fifties-style summer dress depicting enormous brightly-coloured blooms and boasting a white hat and gloves. Gloves! She looked like a negative of Doris Day. Shirley watched, entranced, as the woman tottered off to the Ladies. There was something in her gait that told her she was upset, possibly crying. Paul stayed in his seat.

Shirley felt a sudden urge to pee.

"Alasdair. Traci. Come on! Put your heads together. I'm just off to the loo. Work together - nicely. See if you can come up with a name by the time I get back."

Cullen drew back the curtain and stepped out from the mens stockroom. All the lights on the ground floor were now off but there was light seeping down the stairwell from upstairs and Cullen had been listening intently for the last hour or so. No-one had left the building.

Cocking an ear for any sound, he pulled off his hat to hear better and stuffed it into a jacket pocket. Slowly but steadily, he trod towards the staircase and started up.

The light was coming from the stockroom behind the Ladies Shoes section. Cullen peeked through but saw only boxes piled up almost to the ceiling, with a corridor through them. A shadow was being thrown across the corridor at the end of the room and Cullen could hear the faintest tapping of a keyboard. He padded forward, towards the light until he reached a frame with no door, just an alcove off the main stockroom with a desk and chair and a few files on shelves. Bryce's back was to him and whatever he was doing he was lost in it sufficiently to have no idea Cullen was there.

Cullen leant against the door jamb and watched over Bryce's shoulder, waiting.

Shirley stood outside the door to the Ladies and tried to gather her thoughts. This woman she'd seen go inside was young and pretty, slim and shapely, well-dressed and still had gloves on. Shirley's first thought was: what a demure and classy young thing she was. Her second thoughts was: what the hell did she see in Paul?

They say that love is blind, was this young woman? Shirley wasn't. She knew Paul's faults - but, and here was very much the rub, she loved him anyway. How many times had she defended her choice of man against her mother's cruel tongue?

He's lazy!

No, he prioritises work-life balance. He works to live, he very much didn't live to work.

He's forgetful!

No, he's... okay, he is forgetful.

He's a slob!

He is a tradesman who doesn't earn much. Food and heating and a roof over his head would alway trump clothes and personal grooming when it came to spending precious resources like time and money.

He's happy to spend time and money in the Lamb & Flag!

Hmmm, okay. Good point, well made.

On and on it went but the verbal tennis matches, as far as Shirley as concerned, were never straight set victories for her mother. Paul had lots of good points and the time they spent together was fun and comfortable and... oh how she hated the word, *nice.* Okay, he could do with losing a bit of weight, then so could she; but he had a heart of gold, and a good word for everyone. He was kind and caring and gentle and... dammit, he was hers! Paul was her lover and partner and... okay, project. And, yes, his healthcare needed addressing. She thought she'd had all that in hand with their vegetarian diet thing and trying to reduce his gout... ah but, that was where it had all gone wrong. And that was why she was not with him tonight.

She knew he'd been coming in to Greggs to talk to her; and God knows how many times she'd popped in to the Lamb & Flag looking for him only to be told by Davy that he wasn't in. It was obvious they were meant to be together, but she had to admit that they were both proud and stubborn, each felt let down by the other. They both needed time to realise that and make gentle approaches towards each other so that they could reconnect and heal.

How much time? Who knew. But if Paul was going to be using that time with this young... floozy! Then, well, there would be no healing or reconnecting. There'd be severing, maiming and merry hell to pay!

Shirley took a deep breath and pushed on into the toilets.

Charles was rapt as he reviewed the footage on his laptop. The cup of tea he'd made for himself was going cold, forgotten in the china cup and saucer in his hand.

Entranced by the sight of this ebony goddess in his changing room, Charles felt his pulse speed. He put the cup and saucer down to stop them shaking.

The harsh light of the changing room made her shoulders and arms gleam and shine like some perfectly waxed bodywork, showroom fresh. She had her back to the camera but it didn't matter to Charles. He had seen this all live anyway. This was the editted highlights, his Match Of The Day, with endless slow-motion, freeze frame and unlimited time for analysis. All that was missing was the heady scent he had detected from her, but his memory filled that in for him as he watched, the fragrance returning to him as vividly as that long-lost smell of his exotic childhood neighbour.

He reached for the mouse and, hearing a sound behind him, whirled in his seat. The tramp with the awful hat was leaning against the doorway, a curious glint in his eye.

"What the hell do you think you are doing here? Get out! We're closed and this is private property."

"It's private alright." The tramp gestured with his chin to the monitor still displaying the changing room footage and Charles wheeled and tried to slam the lid of his laptop down. A strong hand stopped him.

"Get out this minute or I'll-"

The tramp grabbed Charles by the jacket lapel. "What?"

"I'll... I'll... call the Police. Don't you threaten me. I'm a freeman of the burgh. I am the proprietor of this store. I'm-"

"A pervert." The tramp ripped the badge from Charles's lapel and rolled it in his fingers, the metal pin gleaming in the low light. "And a Ministerial Servant."

Charles' blinked furiously. "Yes! Yes, I am a Ministerial Servant. I am a member of the church - although what that's got to do you with you I do not know."

"We'll come on to that." The tramp grabbed Charles by the throat and from nowhere produced a roll of duct tape.

Charles' eyes grew and he tried to lash out, writhing in his chair as the tramp manhandled him and the tape. For an old vagrant he had a strong grip and Charles' slender frame was all too pliable.

"Help! Help! Police!" He cried out only to find a hard hand smash into his mouth.

"We'll come on to them too. Probably."

Before he knew it Charles was strapped to his chair. He started to sob quietly.

"Please, what do you want? Let me go, you can have money. There's a day's takings in the safe. I know the combination."

"I don't want your money."

Oh good, thought Charles.

"I want to know about Malcolm Baxter."

Oh shit, thought Charles.

Shirley approached the young woman in the Ladies - a girl, really - dabbing her eyes in the mirror with a scrunched-up piece of toilet tissue. The woman looked at Shirley's reflection and forced a smile. She had tremendous teeth - what was it with people today, all these perfect teeth? Shirley unconsciously curled her lips a little bit tighter together to conceal her own.

"Has he upset you?"

The young woman nodded and re-dabbed her eyes.

"He took the name of Our Lod Jeez U in vain." She sniffed. "Twice."

Shirley's eyes widened. "Yes, well, he's like that. Not

religious *at all*."

This woman and Paul were really not going to get on. Shirley smiled to herself and reached into her handbag for a handkerchief.

"Thank you." She took Shirley's offering and popped the damp toilet paper into a bin. "I understand, um... atheism? Isaiah explained it to me. In my country we do not have it, but here... yes, I know it is here."

"Your country?"

"Ghana. I am from Ghana." She gave a beaming smile, her wet eyes making it seem brighter and even more enormous.

"Here on holiday, then?" Shirley asked, hopefully.

"No. Isaiah brought me here to help him create his church in Scotland."

"Here?"

"Yes. On North Street. Paul came to find me there."

"Paul came to your church?" Shirley's eyes came out on stalks.

"Yes. And I agreed to come here with him."

"Wow." Was all Shirley could manage. She had so many questions. Uppermost was the one she posed: "Why?"

That smile again. "He is building a cross. For our Easter cele-*bray*-shone."

"A cross? But he's not religious!"

"No. But he is kind."

"Aye." Said Shirley then, under her breath. "When he wants to be. When he wants to get into your knickers."

"Excuse me?"

"Nothing."

"He helped me choose this dress!" She did a little pirouette and made the skirt billow out in a flurry of red and yellow flowers.

Shirley blinked. Paul *hated* shopping. He had never helped her choose an outfit - probably because his taste ran to the bloody awful. Although, fair play, she did look marvellous in her new outfit. Shirley tried to re-focus on the matter in hand.

"Aye... but... well... taking the Lord's name in vain though? I mean, that says a lot about a man doesn't it, hmm?"

"Yes. It does." The woman looked downcast and dabbed her eyes again.

"Says he can't be trusted."

"No. And he swears. A lot. That is not nice. It is disrespectful."

"You're right. It is. That, if you don't mind me saying so, is a relationship red flag right there."

The young woman took a deep breath and sighed. "He chooses his friends poorly."

"I'm sure." Shirley said, far from sure what this woman meant. Was this a quote from the bible? "The Lord, do you mean?"

"Thee Lod?"

"Yes. Does he choose his friends poorly?"

"No, not at all." The woman was suddenly filled with evangelical fervour. "Thee Lod chooses those who are righteous and humble themselves before Him."

"Right." Shirley wrinkled her nose, confused.

"But Mister Slasher is a very rude man."

"Yes, he-. Sorry, who?"

"Mister Slasher."

"Is that what Paul told you his name was?"

"No." Now the young woman wrinkled her nose. "I do not know Paul's surname."

"Hmm." Shirley narrowed her eyes. "Another red flag

- what's he hiding? I'd stay well away if I were you."

The young woman composed herself in the mirror and returned Shirley's handkerchief. She straightened her back.

"You know this man?"

"Paul?"

"Mister Slasher."

"Well, yes. But that's not his name, really."

"Ah yes." She nodded. "It is his... nickname."

"Paul's nickname is Mister Slasher?"

"No." The young woman laughed, her white skullcap dazzling Shirley from the reflected the ceiling light. "Mister Slasher's real name is... Kenny!"

"What?" Shirley was royally confused. "Who the f-, heck is Kenny?"

"Kenny is Paul's friend. Very rude man."

"And you're here with Kenny?"

"No, I am here with Paul!"

"On a date?"

"No. We are just friends. I told you, he is building a cross for us."

"Us?"

"Isaiah and me!"

"And Isaiah is your husband?" The woman shook her head. "Partner?"

"No. Isaiah is my pastor!"

Of course, thought Shirley. Clear as bloody mud.

The young woman took one final glance in the mirror and, happy with what she saw, smiled a farewell at Shirley and left the Ladies. Shirley stood, gazing emptily at herself in the mirror, wondering what the hell she had just achieved, if anything.

SEVEN

Quiz Night was one of the few sacrosanct cornerstones in Paul's calendar and, hence, capitalised. Ever since Davy had introduced the idea a couple of years back, Paul had shown an intense, surprising, competitiveness - surprising given that his own personal stash of general knowledge (small to begin with and subsequently tainted and corrupted by the dubious additions and fabrications osmotically absorbed from Davy himself) had now shrunk to the point where his personal contributions to his team's score each week were best unremarked upon. But for Paul, the Quiz Night represented one of the few chances in life to be a winner and he would rather not dwell on the fact that he was hanging on the coat-tails of his team mates rather than deserving to share the podium with them.

Not that they often won.

But it was his team and he was captain. That was all anyone needed to know.

Perhaps it was, in fact, credit to Paul's captaincy that his team was ever victorious at all - given its makeup. Paul hadn't so much as curated or hand-picked the members, more engulfed them into participation, like some drunken sunbathers who had been swept off the beach and plunged into the pool by a sudden tsunami.

While Blessing was still absent, his two missing team members turned up.

First to arrive was Scott The Postman, a big beefy highlander, all freckles and muscle and ginger hair who always wore his Royal Mail uniform, on or off duty. No-one had ever seen Scott in anything other than a red shirt (short-sleeved to expose his muscular arms and thick wrists), short trousers (to best display his tanned, hairy calves like the steel cables from the Forth Road Bridge), thick woollen socks and beige Timberland boots. If the weather got really bad, Scott would throw on a gilet and baseball cap. Job done.

He was always referred to as Scott The Postman, even to his face, although his real name was Scott Lang - short for Scottish Language, Paul reckoned. Scott's specialist subject: music, particularly the music of The Clash.

Paul was telling Scott The Postman about Blessing when Wee Jamie McPherson finally appeared.

"What time do you call this, then?" growled Kenny.

Jamie dropped into his seat, wiping his veiny nose with nicotine-stained fingers. "Ach. Been havin' a bit of trouble." He was a small, grey, wiry terrier of a bloke with a disproportionately large head - a sniper's dream, Slasher said - who lived in a residential caravan park on the outskirts of town with his wife, Joan. Jamie pointed to her now, standing at the bar.

"She's not on our team tonight, is she?" Slasher asked in alarm.

"Fuck no." Said Jamie. "She's wi' The Enemy."

There was a audible intake of breath from all around the table. *The Enemy* was code for a team of teachers who regularly swept the board at The Pub Quiz. Their team size varied in number from week to week but had recently been capped to six after Paul had lodged an "official complaint". It had been a tough call for Davy, because The

Teachers had initially arrived by the busload and waded their way through a whole case of Pinot Grigio, and Prosecco when they won, which wasn't to be sniffed at. But no amount of wine consumption was going to replace his profit margin if the likes of Paul and his mates found another watering hole.

"We do have an extra team member tonight, mind." Paul piped up. The others looked at Wee Jamie to gauge his reaction. Jamie looked around for this new addition but, seeing no-one, narrowed his eyes.

"You windin' me up agin?"

"No, straight up. She's in the Ladies. Be back soon."

"A woman?"

"Aye. Friend of mine."

"She's black." Offered Kenny. "From Afric-aaaaah."

Paul flashed Kenny a nasty look but Jamie seemed unfazed. "I dinna mind tha'. But is she any guid? I'm a bit short the now and if she improves our chances, like, I'm all for it, ken?"

Jamie scratched a living as a Man With A Van, but was always on the scrounge. His nom-de-quiz - The Exorcist - had been acquired after Scott The Postman had invited him round to watch a match on his big screen TV one time and, afterwards, noted that by the time Jamie had gone so had all his spirits. Jamie's specialist subject: geography.

"And she's a God Botherer." Kenny added.

Paul jabbed him in the ribs and then looked at Jamie. "Dunno if she's any good, actually. Neither does she, as it goes. She's never done a quiz before."

"Oh, bollocks!" Blurted Kenny. "All we need."

"If you don't shut the fu-! Oh, Hi Blessing. You back, then?"

Blessing stood over the table, shy yet shining. Six eyes around the table goggled at her while Paul did his best to make introductions. He was pleased to see she was smiling and her eyes were dry.

There was a sudden burst of microphone feedback and the distorted voice of Davy came over the speakers. "Right, Ladies and Gentlemen. Pencils at the ready. We going to start, traditionally, with Round One."

Paul shuffled up to let Blessing sit beside him. He smiled stiffly at her but she seemed at ease now so he tried to relax and focus on the quiz.

"Question One: What is Johnny Depp's full name?"

"Is it Jonathon Department?" Traci offered, now midway through her fifth cocktail.

"No, it's not." Spat Alasdair. "Any more than Randy Andy is short for Randrew Andrew."

"Who's Randy Andy?"

"Never mind."

Shirley returned to the table and sat down, trying to smile. Alasdair rebuked her.

"We've already started!"

"Sorry. Got chatting."

"In the toilets?"

"It's what we women do." Traci blurted.

"Yes. Sorry. What have I missed?"

"Only question one. Johnny Depp's full name."

Shirley squinted and then shook her head. "No idea."

"Me neither."

"I do." Traci gave a drunken smile and Alasdair looked at Shirley, deadpan.

"No. You. Don't" He declared.

The tannoy spoke: "Question Two: What was Gandhi's first name?"

"Oh! Goosey Goosey!" Traci blurted.

Alasdair pursed his lips. "No. It's Mahatma."

Traci scowled at him and slurred: "Do you think I'm stupid?"

"Well, I think we may have exhausted all the other possibilities."

"Team, team team!" Shirley clapped her hands, trying desperately to salvage something from the exercise. "Do we have a name, yet then?"

"No."

Shirley closed her eyes. This was all going swimmingly.

"Question One: What do you know about Malcolm Baxter?"

"Never heard of him."

"Never? Prominent local businessman, like yourself; senior member of a family with long history in the area, like yourself; probably a freeman of the burgh, like yourself?"

"Okay. I have heard of him. Don't know him."

"Never shopped here then?"

"Even if he had, doesn't mean I'd know him."

The tramp nodded to the laptop screen. "Seems to me you'd know an awful lot about anyone that shops here."

"I don't know him... as such."

"No? He knew you."

Charles's eyes whirled in his head. What did this thug know and what did he want? "Who says he knew me?"

"He did." The man's nails dug into Charles's skin as he gripped his chin to lock eyes. "And now I am."

Charles swallowed hard. "Honestly, don't know the man."

"He's dead."

"Didn't!" Charles corrected himself, his voice rising in panic. "Didn't know the man!"

The tramp considered this for a moment, maintaining a painful grip on Charles' face. "Okay. We'll come back to that."

Scott The Postman brought a tray of drinks back to their table as Davy's voice wowwed and fluttered through the speaker system.

"Question Four: What is the First Law of Thermodynamics?"

Scott The Postman, Slasher and Wee Jamie all looked at each other. Blessing sat quietly next to Paul.

"Is it *We don't talk about thermodynamics*?" Offered Paul.

Scott The Postman shook his head. "It's something about not being able to create or destroy energy. I think."

"That can't be right." Kenny said. "'Cos if you turn on the fire it gets hot."

"Aye, but you're only converting one sort of energy to another. Like the energy that exists in wood, when you burn it, it becomes heat. But the amount of energy overall stays the same."

Paul nodded, appreciatively. "Sounds like he knows what he's talking about."

"Aye." Agreed Jamie.

"Yeah, but there's several laws of thermodynamics. I don't know which one that is."

"Boll-" Kenny caught Paul's look in time. "I mean... dash it all."

"Let's leave that. Come back to it later."

"Next question", said Cullen. "What do you know about Iain McKenna?"

"Who?" Charles felt the sweat evaporating from his brow. He really didn't know whoever the tramp was on about now.

"McKenna. Iain Nesbitt McKenna."

"No idea."

The tramp was looking from one eye to the other, searching for something. Seemingly not finding it, he asked again.

"Think hard. Iain. Nesbitt. McKenna."

"I think I'd remember that name." Charles managed, the tramp's breath heavy on his face.

"You don't know Baxter. You don't know McKenna. Is it possible that you are just some innocent Ministerial Servant, I wonder?"

"Yes! I am, I am!" Charles gasped, delighted that sense was beginning to prevail.

"Huh."

"There are lots of us! Ministerial Servants, I mean. There's obviously been some sort of mistake. I'm innocent."

The tramp leant back, relaxing seemingly. "Do you know they call you The Creep?"

"Who?"

"Your staff. Why do you think that is?"

"I don't... they don't! Who says?"

"They say." He stood up straight and looked over his Charles' shoulder at the screen. "Do you think they would call an innocent man *The Creep*?"

"I...I...I..."

"Let's find out shall we?" And he disappeared into the stockroom.

"Round Three: Sport:" wobbled Davy. "In what sport do you hear the terms *jerk* and *snatch*?"

Paul glared at Kenny. "Don't say a bloody word, Slash."

"I wasn't going to!"

"Weightlifting." Wee Jamie piped up.

"Sure?"

"Aye. Definitely."

"Right. We'll have that." Paul scribbled it down on the paper and then smiled at Blessing. "We usually do well at Sport."

"Question Two: What form of physical exercise was invented by, and is named after, a German."

"That's not sport!" Yelled Kenny, only to be drowned out by a group of people shouting "Shut up!" and "Just answer the question!"

"Bloody teachers." He sulked.

"Do you think it could be *Herr Robics*?" Paul asked.

Scott The Postman looked at Paul, dumbfounded. "No. I think it's *pilates*."

"Don't sound German to me." Sniffed Kenny. "Sounds Greek."

"Anyone got any better suggestions?"

The group just muttered to itself so Paul committed their answer to paper.

The heel of the stiletto came down through the back of Charles' hand, pinning him to the table. It felt like he'd had his whole body impaled on a red hot poker and he threw his head back and howled. His hand throbbed and blood bubbled from the wound at the top and oozed out beneath his palm. Soon the table was sticky, the metallic smell strong in the small space.

The tramp pulled the bloody shoe from Charles' hand and he let out another almighty cry and grabbed his hand to him, nursing his fingers as he tried in vain to flex them. His breath came in huge, racking sobs as the pain coursed through him.

The tramp was wiping the heel against the doorframe, contemplating the shoe.

"That's a two hundred pound shoe, that is. According to the box." He hefted it in his hand. "Guess you get what you pay for."

Charles was openly weeping now, great bubbles of snot in his nostrils, gulping for air, his shoulders heaving. The tramp looked on impassively.

"I told you: I don't know anything!"

"Yeah, you did. So let's try again. Now you can see how important it is that I get the right answers."

"I don't know anything!"

"That's not true, though, is it? You do know about Baxter. Maybe not McKenna, but Baxter for sure. I can tell."

"No! I told you. I... wait, what are you doing that f-?"

Charles's question was suffocated by a piece of duct tape over his mouth.

"See, you have another hand." Her jerked his thumb back over his shoulder to the stockroom. "And we have plenty more shoes."

"And the answer to question ten: Name a bird with a long neck..." Davy was giving out the answers at the end of the penultimate round of the quiz. "I will accept *swan, heron, pelican, goose, flamingo, crane, stork*. Any of those."

"What about *Naomi Campbell*?" A drunken voice shouted from the back of the pub.

"No. Right. Final round. And, for those of you new to the quiz, this is the Double Jeopardy round."

There was a sarcastic *oooooh* from all the regulars.

"Like all the other rounds, there are ten questions but, in this round, each correct answer is worth double - ie., two points. But if you get ANY answer wrong, you score NO points for the whole round. So, if you aren't certain of the answer leave it blank rather than risk an answer and lose all the points from this round. Are we ready? Okay, question one: what colour is the black box on an aeroplane?"

Wee Jamie, leant in conspiratorially. "Trick question, innit?"

"Is it?" Paul was all ears. This was the make or break round. Lots of points and many a team in contention at this point could fail due to over-confidence. Correct answers in this round were like gold dust.

"Aye."

"What colour is it then?"

Jamie lowered his voice. "Orange. So's you find it easy in a crash, ye ken?"

"Brilliant." Paul grinned. "Everyone okay with putting that down?"

They all nodded.

"Question Two: What is the collective noun for a group of unicorns?"

"Scottish national animal that." Paul added,

authoritatively.

"Is it? That's bloody brilliant innit? National animal that doesnae exist." Jamie chuckled. "Only us Scots could thinka that, eh?"

"Aye. But what do you call a group of them?" Scott The Postman asked.

"It's another trick question." Said Paul. "You never get a group of them - they're so rare."

"Two trick questions in the same round?" Kenny said. "Doesn't sound like Davy. I think there's a legit answer."

"I know."

They all turned to look at Blessing. She had sat there, demure and polite next to Paul all evening, not saying a word and not asking any questions. And now she had spoken.

"What is it?" asked Paul.

"It's my name! Blessing!" She cried, beaming a huge smile.

"Shhhhh!" Hushed Paul, looking anxiously around lest any other team should hear their answer.

"A blessing of unicorns?" asked Scott The Postman.

"Yes!"

"You sure?"

"Yes!"

"Wow. Okay." Paul was convinced. "Let's write that down."

"Wait a minute-" Kenny put a hand over Paul's and then, seeing the look on his face, instantly withdrew it. "I'm just saying-"

"It's going down."

Everyone dipped their head into the pints and waited for the next question.

Bryce was a blubbering mess, lying slumped over the sticky desk, his blood coagulating into a black-red pool in the dim light. He was moaning in pain, surfing in and out of consciousness.

Cullen watched him with a heavy heart for many minutes realising the man had nothing more to give. He had been convinced there was a connection with Baxter. Seen it in this man's eyes. Felt his heart thump and his mind race with hope.

But it seemed a dead end. False hope.

The man was a pervert and a creep but was he just a random Ministerial Servant? As Bryce himself had said, there were many of them - perhaps thousands of them across the country. What were the chances that this one was *the* one?

But why had Baxter given him that detail? Why, in his very dying breath, had they been the two words which he'd forced through his lips? It didn't make sense. What was he missing?

He grabbed the man's laptop, wiping the lid clean with his sleeve. Maybe there was something in here that would provide a clue.

He turned out the light and crept out through the darkness back into the alley, hugging the laptop to him, head down. All hope pinned on its contents. But, as he well knew, it's the hope that kills you.

"Okay, and the final question for tonight: In which book of the Bible does it say *Unto us a child is born.*"

Paul looked at Blessing and her eyes were alive with delight and joy.

"Do you know it?"

She nodded and beamed her most brilliant smile.

"Here, you write it down then. That way no-one will hear."

Paul shook his head in wonder as she took the pencil from him.

"What are the chances? You see - it's the soup! The soup has provided. It always does."

"Whit you on aboot?" Wee Jamie piped up. "Whit soop?"

"The soup." Paul put up his palms to defer any questions. "Trust me. Trust the soup. It works."

"Aye. Probably a sight more than you do." Kenny shook his head, wearily. "If she ain't right we've just lost all our points."

"Look." Paul explained. "Blessing knows the Bible inside out. Isn't that right?"

"Yes." She nodded enthusiastically. "It is thee Holy Scripture. Thee route to our Lord Jeez U's heart and soul." She turned to Paul. "It is not thee soup, it is Thee Lod! He has brought you here and he has brought me here and he has given us these questions so we may believe in Him!"

Slasher put his pint to his lips and swore under his breath.

"Well, I have no idea." said Scott The Postman. "So, if Blessing is certain..."

"I am. I am!" She gave a little clap of excitement.

"Let's see the answer, then." He pulled the piece of paper towards him and turned it round so he could read it. Blessing's answer was one word.

Isaiah.

Shirley returned to their table with the final drinks order of the night. Her team, less united more untied, had finished nowhere.

"It's woo-woo." Traci insisted.

"No, it's not. It's nee-nah." Alasdair was slurring now.

"Is it bollocks."

"It is."

"It's not. It's woo-woo."

"What the hell is wrong with the pair of you? It's like dealing with four year-olds. Some team-building exercise this turned out to be." Shirley folded her arms and sighed. "Hopefully no-one will question the size of the drinks bill I've just paid."

"Oh, but look on the bright side." Traci, almost inarticulate from drink, goggled at the Flaming Sambucca Shirley had reluctantly placed in front of her. "It's not often I get soiled rotten."

"You mean spoiled rotten?"

"I know what I mean. Haaaaa!!" Traci grinned from ear to ear.

"Well, I am very disappointed." Alasdair ran a perfectly manicured hand shakily through his hair. "We were doing well until that final round."

"I am sorry." Shirley winced. "It was a bad call on my part."

"Not your fault." Alasdair patted her on the hand while giving Traci a killing look. "She can be very insistent."

"Well, there's always next time?"

Alasdair looked at her askance and hiccoughed. "You want to do this again?"

"Not really." Shirley was downcast. "I was trying to bring us together. Make us a more effective team. This didn't work... and I don't have any other ideas right now."

"What about paintballing?"

"Um. I hear that really hurts - if you get hit?"

"Yes, it does." Alasdair shot another look at Traci.

Shirley sighed and looked over at Paul's team, jubilant at their victory. "I guess they had the edge on us anyway."

"Well, I assume they come here every week. This was our first time."

"There is that. But I was thinking more about their bible knowledge."

Alasdair turned to look at the strange mix of individuals that made up the winning team: a burly postman, a large tattooed rugby player, a small weasel of a man who looked ill, and a beautiful young black woman in a white hat and gloves.

"Which one's the biblical scholar then?"

"The young lady." Shirley said. "Very devout."

"You know her?" He studied her again, having difficulty focussing. "Can't say I've seen here before."

"No, she's new. Friend of Paul's."

"Oh, so where's he, then? He's always coming in looking for you."

"I know." Shirley tightened her lips and nodded towards the bar. "He's over there. And he can away and boil his head."

Alasdair smiled and patted her hand again. "You know, you can do so much better than him."

"Can I though?"

"Yes. Yes you can." He looked her in the eye. "Wait here."

"Where you off to?"

But Alasdair stood and strode, somewhat unsteadily, towards the bar.

"Come on then, Davy. My team's getting thirsty!"

Paul was tapping on the bar while he waited for Davy to finish his drinks order. The winning prize was £100 worth of free booze and Paul wanted to dive head-first into plenty, big style. Davy's head appeared from under the counter with a bottle of Pomagne which he uncorked loudly.

"Well, you surprised me good and proper, Beep, I tell you. Never had you lot down as religious types."

"Eh?"

"Isaiah. That last question? That was the one wot won it for you."

"Yeah? Well, that was our new star player - Blessing. She's big on all that."

"Right, well there you go. There's almost fifty quid on here."

Davy placed the bottled down on a tray already holding two very tall, colourful drinks with umbrellas in them, a couple of double whiskies and four dark pints. He made the sign of the cross over it. "In nomine Patris et Baileys et Spirits & Mixers"

"Wha?" Paul was bemused.

"It's a joke." Said a voice behind him. "Bit like yourself."

Paul turned to find himself being addressed by the young Liberace from Greggs. Under these spotlights above the bar, this close up, he looked particularly shiny. Paul wondered if spent his free time taking shiny lessons.

"Well, I mean. Don't suppose you've ever read the bible, have you?" Asked Liberace.

"No."

"Well I have." He boasted. "And let me tell you, it's full

of such stuff - you wouldn't believe!"

"Not now, mate." Paul picked up the tray and headed back to his table. Liberace followed him, talking over his shoulder.

"See I went to Sunday School as a nipper. We got told all these stories and some of 'em, really cool when you're a nipper. So I'd go home and scour the Bible for more. Didn't want to wait a week for the next episode."

"Alasdair, leave it?" This was Shirley who had appeared at his shoulders and was now looking, shame-faced, at Paul with a grimace on her face.

"Even I was shocked." Alasdair said, oblivious. "And I don't shock easy."

Paul placed the tray down at his table to noisy acclaim and started allocating drinks, hoping if he ignored this Alasdair he'd go away. He certainly hadn't bargained on Shirley coming this close to Blessing. Suddenly he felt strangely exposed.

"Maybe we could chat about this later, hmm?"

"Why don't we ask her?" Alasdair slurred, nodding at Blessing. "See if she has, you know, a different interpretation. On the scriptures, like?"

Before Paul could respond, Alasdair turned to address her.

"What do you think about Lot then?"

"Excuse me?"

"Lot. And his wife?"

"Oh, yes please. She is turned into a pillar of salt by Thee Lod."

"Correct." Alasdair nodded proudly to Paul and then turned again to Blessing. "Why?"

Blessing blinked, several times. "Because she looked back. She disobeyed Thee Lod."

"Correct again. Well done. Incidentally, what was her name?"

"Her name?"

"Aye. What was the name of Lot's wife?"

"I'm afraid-"

"Anyone?" Alasdair looked around the now silent group with an annoyingly confident air. "No, it's okay. God Bless You. You won't know it because she didn't have one. Well, I say she didn't have one. Obviously she had one - everyone has a name don't they? But the Bible neglects to tell us what it was. 'Cos she only has a walk-on part I guess. Second pillar of salt on the right, kind o' thing."

Alasdair turned his attention back to Blessing. "His daughters don't have names either, do they? Funny that. It's almost like God doesn't think women are important enough to have names. Not proper people, like."

Blessing sat with a rictus smile while Paul looked on, lost for words.

"But they're useful plot points, aren't they? And damned useful sex objects." Alasdair leered at her, all smooth veneer gone.

"Alright, pal. That's enough." Scott The Postman pushed himself forward in his chair. "I think you've had enough to drink. Blessing is new here, let's play nice, eh?"

"I'm only quoting the Bible, postie. It's all there in black and white. Isn't that right, Blessing? Nice name, that. And, see, Lot was blessed. God sent a couple of angels to stay with him. In Sodom, which is where he lived. Not the nicest of areas, but what can you do? Anyway, the people of Sodom seem to have a thing for angels, 'cos they turn up en masse like, and threaten to beat down Lot's door unless he lets them all rape the angels he's got staying with him. This is anal rape, by the way - hence the name Sodom."

Shirley put her arm on his shoulder and tried to pull him back. "Alasdair, will you come away!"

Paul was stunned, watching Shirley now almost wrestling with Alasdair to get him away from the table.

"Now Lot, not wanting to offend Him, isn't too keen on handing over two of God's chosen beings to a load of arse bandits so he offers his two nameless daughters to the mob instead. And, sweetens the deal, by letting them know that they're both virgins! What a gent! But, see, the mob's got its heart set on some anal angel action so they decline, whereupon the angels turn up and blind them all! And they call down God's vengeance on the city and He sets about destroying it."

"I said, play nice." Scott The Postman threatened. "Maybe you could just apologise to Blessing and-"

"For what? For telling her what she already knows? What's in her favourite book?" Alasdair sneered and continued. "So, Lot and his daughters and his wife have to leg it and God warns them not to look back in case they see the nastiness he gets up to slaughtering the whole bloody population - women and children - just because the blokes all got a bit over-excited. But, oh dear! What are women like? Because Lot's wife won't do as she's told, will she? She knows better. She's dying for a good nosy, so she turns round to have a butcher's at all the blood and gore and God turns her into a pillar of salt!"

"I'm waiting for that apology." Scott The Postman said, his face dark.

"Right. I'll put it in the post, that way you'll never get it."

"Alasdair!" Shirley, realising wrestling with him wasn't

working, had resorted to her managerial voice, but Alasdair was too far gone.

"Will you let go of me?" He wrenched her arm from his shoulder and Shirley cried out in pain.

Paul's punch sent him halfway across the room.

EIGHT

The barking of dogs hazily penetrated Paul's skull and he wanted to mumble some instruction for them to quieten down when he felt a hand over his mouth. He shot up in bed

"Jesus Christ!"

"It's me." Whispered Cullen.

Paul exhaled loudly, clutching a hand to his chest. "Shit! What'd you do that for?"

"Wake you?"

"No - put your hand over my mouth."

"Precautions."

"Right."

Cullen turned the light on and Paul cried out, shielding his eyes. Ant and Dec, perhaps now recognising Cullen, wandered off into the unlit living room.

"Heavy night?" Cullen asked.

"Celebratin' weren't I?"

"Snoring's what you were doing. Took a lot to wake you."

"Pardon me, Mister Come In Here And Wake Me Without Permission. I wasn't expecting I'd have to get up in the middle of the night." He uncovered his eyes slowly and squinted at Cullen. "What time is it?"

"Late."

"You mean early." Paul now fully awake, stared at his

friend. "Is that blood?"

Cullen glanced down at his jacket. It looked like he'd been butchering a stag. "It's not mine."

"Pleased to hear it. Anyone I know?"

"Charles Bryce."

"You're joking!"

"No."

"Shit! What've have you-?"

"He's alright. Just sustained a flesh wound or two."

Paul scanned Cullen's hands and clothing. "Only two?"

"Look, you can catch up on the details later. Right now, I need you to give me a hand."

"Ah. Could be a problem there." Paul gingerly brandished his right hand, bruised and swollen.

"What'd you do?"

"Er. Hit some... thing. Hard." He grinned sheepishly.

"Is that what you were celebrating?"

"No. Yes. No. You can catch up on the details later."

"Right. Well, not to worry. I don't need dexterity, just heft."

"Well, heft is my middle name." Paul yawned. "Can we do this in the morning?"

Cullen leant down and put his face into Paul's. "No. Listen, I helped you with an after-dark job so you can now help me. One hand washes the other."

"Yeah, but that was for a cross."

"This is for a cross."

Paul boggled. "You putting up a cross 'n' all?"

"No. I want to decorate yours."

The next morning, Blessing and Isaiah strode out into the spring sunshine, heading to the High Street to commence their morning's work. The air was fresh, the sky was blue and bright blossoms shimmered on the trees.

As Isaiah rounded the corner he stopped suddenly and Blessing, who had been scurrying to keep up with his brisk pace, ran right into him. Startled she looked first at him and then followed his gaze.

"Hallelujah! Praise Thee Lod!" Isaiah cried, shaking his head in disbelief. He dropped down to his knees and raised his eyes to heaven, arms aloft. "Lod Jeez U we beseech you! On this day of days, how blessed are we to celebrate your eternal life."

His eyes were white and wild with delight. "Do you see, my child? Do you see?"

Blessing gazed upon the scene in front of her. On the traffic island in front of Bryce & Sons was Isaiah's cross. Standing proudly, illuminated by a shaft of sunlight as if Thee Lod himself was showering His favour upon it. A large crowd was gathered, looking up, animated, marvelling. From her vantage point she could only see the rear of the cross but the sound of their chatter cascaded all around, bouncing off the walls of the shops on the High Street.

"Our brother Paul, His carpenter, has delivered to us a worthy centre piece. Let us embrace thee multitude and gather them to us in cele-bray-shone in thee name of Lod Jeez U."

Isaiah rose to his feet and clutched her hand. Blessing felt the energy and strength from her pastor surging through her like some divine bolt of electricity. Together they crossed the road and closed in on the throng, gathered in wonderment.

Suddenly, from her right came the sound of sirens. Two police cars turned onto the High Street and screeched to a halt in the middle of the road. A policewoman jumped out and started directing traffic away down South Street while her colleagues began laying out cones and a yellow diversion sign. One of the policemen opened his car boot and retrieved a large roll of blue and white tape.

Oblivious to these new arrivals, evangelical fervour in his eyes, Isaiah pushed ahead. Closer to the crowd now, Blessing could sense a different mood - not awe and wonderment, but concern and shock. Voices rose and fell and bodies pressed in from all sides as Isaiah struggled to forge a path through the gathering. She felt an urge to pull back but Isaiah's grip was strong and she found herself being dragged along.

As they came up level with the cross, Isaiah stopped and Blessing gaped at what she saw.

There was a man on the cross, crucified! He had black tape across his mouth and his arms were similarly taped to the cross at the wrists. He was bound at the waist and ankles by the same tape holding him in place. His head hung down and he appeared conscious but too weak to move.

"Come on, move along now. Nothing to see here." The policewoman was trying to disperse the crowd, to little effect. Whatever one could say about the situation, the fact was that there was plenty to see here and the crowd knew it.

"Move along, please!"

Blessing looked questioningly at Isaiah who had dropped her hand and stood blinking up at the man on the cross. Suddenly, he darted into the back of the crowd, pushing his way noisily to the front. Blessing dived in after him, head down, before the hole around him closed.

When he came to a halt, she stopped too and stared up, struggling with the brutal sight before her.

The man's hands were pierced in both palms, his fingers and wrists encrusted with blood. Stigmata! Above his head was a string bag containing two red high heel shoes, also covered in blood and around his neck was a thin chain bearing what looked like a USB stick. At the top of the cross was a sign, handwritten in marker pen on a piece of cardboard. It read: *Servants Of The Lord - Be Sure Your Sins Shall Find You Out.*

As she gazed at the semi-naked figure, he raised his head weakly and she could see it was the man who had sold her the sandals in the department store.

Goosebumps rose on her skin and she felt the hubbub around her drop away, a fog of muddy sound dampening this grisly scene. It was as if the sun had gone in and darkness blanketed everything. Words and phrases from the crowd surfaced through the murk: *The Creep... liked to leer and ogle... groped they say... always gave me the heebs.*

She examined this man's tortured face. There were tracks of tears, encrusted blood, matted hair, bruises. What she was seeing, she realised, was a shocking glimpse into the many horrific punishments meted out in the Holy Book; a real-life, graphic, grotesque depiction of her Lord Jesu's fate.

She felt her hand grasped anew and looked down to find Isaiah's hand on hers, his knuckles white against her skin.

"My child, we must go."

Blessing was roused from her reflection. "Why? Where?"

"Away. From here. Now." He pulled her through the crowd and started dragging her back along the road in the direction of their church.

"Why? Where are we going?"

"This town is not safe. For him. For us. Look at what they've done!"

"But our Easter cele-*bray*-shone!"

"Thee Lod will understand."

"But why is it not safe for us?"

"We do not belong here. We are not wanted here." Isaiah looked into her eyes. "We are in danger here."

"I don't understand."

"My child: one day you will. Come."

"But where are we going?"

"We shall find another town. Somewhere where we are not so... unwelcome."

"But-"

"Come along!" He yanked her arm and she almost lost her footing. Scrambling to keep up with him, she slipped and her hand broke free. Isaiah glanced back to beckon her.

"Come on!"

Blessing stood her ground, blinking.

"Blessing!" He pleaded.

She took a deep breath and slowly let it out. "I need to say goodbye first."

"To who?"

"Wait for me at the church." And she turned and disappeared back into the crush.

"I wonder what's going on over there?" Traci craned her neck trying to see out of the Greggs window when she heard the siren. "There's an ambulance there now."

"Never you mind what's going on, help me get these

customers served." Shirley bristled, trying to wrap four separate breakfast roll orders while juggling coffee cups. Breakfast was one of their busiest times and her she was short-handed - she didn't expect to see Alasdair in today, if ever again, and Traci was clearly the worse for wear judging by the way she'd applied her eyeliner.

"Its Mister Bryce." Said a little old lady at the counter, nodding her head at the window. "Up on a cross he is."

"On a what?"

"Cross. You know, like crucifixion?" She leant in as if to confide in Shirley. "They call him *The Creep* apparently. Doesn't surprise me. Always seemed a bit off. But that's what they say."

"Who's they?"

"People in the crowd. They're all talking about it. It's all they're talking about."

"Aye, well. Probably some student prank or something." Shirley bustled. "Traci, can you refill this machine please? And we're out of milk again."

"No. It's real. There's blood and everything."

Shirley stopped what she was doing and looked up at the old lady. "Blood?"

"Oh aye. It's terrible."

Shirley strode around the counter and went to the window but all she could see was the back of people's heads and then the side of an ambulance blocking her view.

"Let the police deal with it, I say." She got back behind the counter and wiped her hands on her tabard. "Now then, what can I get you?"

The old lady looked about her. "No Alasdair today, then?"

Shirley glared at her but said nothing.

The frantic knocking kept on and on until Paul had crawled out of bed and opened his door to find Blessing standing right in front of him, looking up with big brown eyes. She was wearing the same outfit as last night but in the morning sunshine she looked even more radiant and alive.

"I have come to say goodbye." She wore a sad smile and her eyes were moist.

"Wow, okay." Paul said, trying to wipe the sleep from his eyes. "Do you want a cup of coffee?"

"No, thank-you."

"Mind if I have one?" And he shuffled off into his kitchen unbothered by her reply. "Where are you going?" he called from the dark interior. Out on the deck, Blessing was bathed in glorious light.

"I don't know. Isaiah will tell me."

"Will he? Right-o." He came back out and took a huge gulp of morning air. "When are you off, then?"

"Now. He is waiting for me at the church."

"Oh." His head and his eyes hurt. He kept blinking trying to clear his brain. "Er, wait a minute. He hasn't paid me for the cross!"

"I am sorry. Thee Lod will provide."

"Yeah, right. That's what he said. What the Lord *might* provide won't keep me in beer, will it?"

"Thee Lod provided last night, did he not? He gave us the questions and answers to my prayers."

"Ach. First off: I can't live off questions and answers. Second off: you say Lord, I say soup."

"Does it matter?"

"'Course it matters! Whilst I do, indeed, trust the soup

I don't rely on it for my bread and butter." Paul wiped his nose with one hairy forearm. "That's asking a bit much o' the soup is that."

"Lord Jeez U said: *I am the bread of life; he who comes to Me will not hunger, and he who believes in Me will never thirst.*"

"Aye. But didn't he also say man cannot live on bread alone?"

Blessing blinked slowly, the shovel of his question pinging harmlessly off the bedrock of her faith. She pursed her lips. "You are a good man, Big Paul. Thee Lod will save and protect you."

"Can't you just ask Him to give me the money I'm owed? Today, preferably."

She smiled benevolently and then sank to her knees in front of him. She reached for his crotch and Paul stepped back, appalled.

"What are you doing?"

Blessing looked up at him, still smiling. "Thee Lod's wok."

Paul shook his head, confusion and disbelief written on his face. "No, Blessing. No. Please get up."

"What is wrong?"

"No." Was all he could repeat, shaking his huge head from side to side. He reached down and pulled her back up to her feet. She was as light and fragrant as a summer meadow.

"I don't understand." Blessing bit her lip. "I do thee Lod's wok for Isaiah all thee time."

Paul's face was like thunder. "I think you'd better go."

"But..."

"Now."

Blessing bowed her head and spoke quietly. "I will ask Isaiah to send you the money he owes you."

"I don't want his money." Paul's voice was cold and heavy. "And I don't want to ever see him again."

Blessing started to cry. "Goodbye Big Paul. Beep. I will pray for you."

"Bye." Paul said, numbly, and watched her go, stepping in her gleaming white sandals, down the stoney path, until she was out of sight.

Paul brought his hammer down on the loose piece of deck railing, knocking the final nail firmly into place but wincing at the pain in his hand. The sun was going down and it was starting to turn cold, so he briefly stood to admire his handiwork before retreating inside. The kitchen window behind him fell out of its frame and shattered on the deck.

"Bollocks!"

"You've made a poor fist of that." Cullen's voice came out of nowhere, swiftly followed by the man himself who poked his head around the corner of the cabin.

"Would you, by any chance, care to become acquainted with my poor fist?"

"No."

"Then shut up." Paul exhaled sourly, puffing out his cheeks. He shook his huge head. "Knew I shouldn't have used that mastic. Thought it had gone off."

"It's a poor carpenter who blames his tools."

"Yeah? Well, I am that poor carpenter. Look: carpenter? Poor? *C'est moi*." Paul laid his hammer down and thrust his hands into the pockets of his jogging bottoms.

"Yes, well, I don't think you can blame your poverty on your tools."

"The bible doesn't lie, mate. 'Sonly bloody preachers that lie." He sighed and looked imploringly at Cullen. "Don't suppose you could lend me a few quid, could you?"

"Thought you'd be flush. Getting paid for the Lords' work?"

"What'd you say?" Paul glowered and the outside temperature seemed to drop a few more degrees.

"You know, making that cross." Cullen squinted at the sudden darkness in his friend's face. "What's up?"

"What do you know about Isaiah?"

"Who's Isaiah?"

"That pastor bloke who wanted the cross."

Cullen shook his head. "Nothing. Why?"

"Doesn't matter. Done a runner, is all." Paul said. "I am, not for the first time, potless."

"Ah. Still..." Cullen brightened. "Could be worse."

"How?"

"At least you don't have to wear a stupid hat." Cullen pointed his own headgear.

"Aye well, there is that. You do know you don't have to either?"

"Aye. Kinda growing on me, though."

"Really?" Paul surveyed the picture in front of him. "Looks to me like a kinder egg has vomited on you. So, can you?"

"What?"

"Lend us a few quid."

"What for?"

Paul grinned sheepishly. "Gonna buy Shirley an Easter egg."

"Oh. This is..."

"What?"

"Unexpected." Cullen scratched his nose. "What turn

of events has caused this?"

Paul turned his bruised hand over, examining it. "I just thought... might be a nice gesture 'n' that."

"An olive branch?"

"'Aye."

Cullen eyed his friend and smiled, reaching into a pocket. "Here's twenty."

"Twenty!" Paul's eyes lit up. "I wanna buy her an egg not a farmyard!"

"Well, buy her a good one." Paul's face told Cullen he might need to elaborate further. "An expensive one."

Paul nodded and took the bank note before Cullen added: "And perhaps you could do me a little favour."

"I'm assuming this is for you?"

"Hmm?" Shirley was busy peeling potatoes at the sink when her Mum came into the kitchen.

"This." She was holding out a supermarket carrier bag with both hands. "It was at the door."

Shirley took it, intrigued. "It's heavy. Who's it from?"

Her Mum gave her a considered look and paused for a moment. "No idea."

Shirley wiped her hands on the tea towel and sat down at the kitchen table. She peeled the carrier bag open to reveal an enormous, elaborately decorated chocolate egg nestling inside a basket of smaller eggs. Written on the large egg in white chocolate was a single word.

Soz.

Shirley stared at it for several seconds before, wordlessly, she pulled out a handkerchief from her apron and burst into tears.

MINISTERIAL SERVANT ISN'T WHAT YOU THINK IT IS.

Detective Chief Superintendent Kate Lorimer picked up her phone off the desk and looked at the text message. There was no signature, no sign-off, but her address book had labelled it indelibly: Cullen. Never one for the niceties of conversation.

She gave a little smile, despite herself. The medium of texting, spartan and remote, actually quite suited him. She wondered if he knew.

I KNOW. WHERE ARE YOU?

She waited but the phone sat silently in her hand as she brushed it lightly with her thumb. At least he used his phone now. Some stupid brick of a thing. That suited him too: a throwback. Unfashionable, solid, hard-wearing, but effective.

When she had last spoken to him, Cullen had mentioned the dying words on the lips of Sir Malcolm Baxter: *ministerial servant*. Words Cullen had wrung out of him - she didn't want to know how. Initially she had assumed this was some generic term unlikely to yield anything promising. The Metropolitan Police investigation christened Operation Merlin had embraced so many politicians, civil servants and high-ranking officials such a clue seemed of little use. But a quick Google had turned up the Jehovah's Witness angle so her pulse had quickened at the prospect of a meaningful focus for her enquiries. Until she learnt that there were over 1,500 congregations across the UK, each having several Ministerial Servants. There was no way she was going to authorise that search for a needle in a haystack - just think of the bloody overtime!

No reply forthcoming from the phone, she tried again.

WHERE ARE YOU?

BUSY.

DOING WHAT?

There was another long pause before he responded. When it finally arrived, she realised she'd been holding her breath.

I HAVE SOMETHING :-)

What the...? Had he actually used a smiley face emoji? He bloody had! My God. She shook her head.

TELL ME MORE.

There was something about the man which drew you in. You couldn't put your finger on it. Maybe it was his focus. His earnestness. His ferocity. Whatever it was, you found yourself wanting to know more.

CAN'T.

WHY NOT?

BUSY.

Kate raised her eyes to the ceiling and let out a silent scream. The bloody man was a torment.

GIVE ME A FUCKING CLUE!

The response was instant:

LANGUAGE.

She pursed her lips together.

PLEASE?

Sitting with one leg crossed over the other, she dangled a shoe from her left foot and wiggled it impatiently.

NOT OVER THE PHONE.

COME IN THEN.

The door opened and her sergeant, Jenkins, poked his head into her office.

"Ma'am?"

"Yes?" She snapped.

"Sorry, Ma'am. Mr McInnes wants to see you."

"Paul McInnes?"

"Yes, Ma'am."

"Is here?"

"Yes, Ma'am."

The phone vibrated in her hand and she looked down at it. The message was short. Again.

NO.

She looked up at her Sergeant and sighed. "Bring him in."

Big Paul sauntered in, looking around the room as if a career in quantity surveying beckoned. It didn't. He was wearing plaster-spattered overalls, muddy workboots and a sheepish look. He had both hands behind his back.

"It wasn't me." He volunteered.

Kate narrowed her eyes. "What wasn't?"

"Dunno." Paul grinned, massive teeth gleaming in an almost mahogany face. "Just thought I'd get that on the table, 'fore we started like."

"Why are you here? I don't remember sending for you."

"You didn't."

"So...?"

"I'm here with a message."

"Are you some kind of carrier pigeon?"

The phone buzzed again in her hand before he could answer.

IS HE THERE YET?

Kate frowned at the screen and then looked up at Paul.

"Okay. Let's hear it."

POSTSCRIPT

Charles Aloysius Bryce was treated in Borders General for blood loss, dehydration and hand wounds. He was arrested and charged under Section 9 of the Sexual Offences (Scotland) Act 2009 and is awaiting trial. After providing a statement about his own assault, police are on the lookout for a tramp wearing an orange and brown hat bearing a £7.99 price tag.

Isaiah Bempah Nathaniel Okeke is being sought on suspicion of theft and money laundering. Four branches of The Global Light Revival Ministry for Renewed Christian Fellowship in Scotland have been investigated and their assets frozen.

Blessing Cherish Mnangwa is somewhere in Scotland, whereabouts unknown, doing *Thee Lod's Wok* with Isaiah.

Shirley Stevenson has texted Paul to thank him for the Easter Egg apology and ask him if he would like to meet for a drink. She hasn't told her mother this.

Alasdair Cater took two days off sick before returning to work sporting heavy facial bruising. He is currently on step two out of four in the Greggs' HR disciplinary procedure and will progress to step three if he adjusts himself near the egg custards.

Traci MacColl is pleased that Alasdair is no longer Shirley's Special One and, in a bid to be promoted to Acting Manager When Necessary, is trying really hard to give more of a toss.

"Big" Paul McInnes never did get paid for constructing the cross but consoles himself with the fact that, after Googling to confirm it, there is no record of Jesus ever being paid for carpentry work either.

Mungo James Cullen has removed the price tag from his hat and is still out there, searching.

AUTHOR'S NOTE

I would like to point out that I bear no ill-will or animosity to the Jehovah's Witness organisation, or indeed, any church or religious organisation anywhere. Any inaccuracies about the faiths and beliefs depicted herein are entirely due to my own atheism and/or insufficient research.

I did contact some members of my local Kingdom Hall to attend the Memorial of Christ's Death (their Good Friday commemoration) for research purposes, but I received no response, waited a whole year for the next one and still got no response. I'd like to use that as an excuse for the enormous time gap between this book and its predecessor, but I can't.

This book is dedicated to Jonathan Temples, the bloke what does my book covers. It feels really weird to me that, until I have a cover image done, each book doesn't actually seem real. They are all just ones and zeros stored up in the cloud until this talented third party is able to turn my initial rough ideas for a cover into the polished finished article. I am continually delighted with them and relieved every time I ask that he is willing to do another one for me. Long may he continue.

Thank you to my Beta readers Deidre M, Mike M, Madeleine N, Pete B and John K - their comments and feedback have meant that this book is much better than it really should have been.

Biggest thanks, as always, go to my partner, Claire, who continues to help make my final output enormously better than my first draft. And who, more importantly, throughout the year off where I dropped the writing ball, never criticised or chivvied or did anything other than give me her full, loving support. For that I am, of course, fully undeserving but enormously grateful.

Finally, could Jesus and Big Paul really be connected? Is *the soup* just another form of religion? If it is, it's all news to me, since none of these parallels or analogies had occurred to me until I started writing this book.

But, whatever you personally believe, please....

Don't write in.

mjf
27.4.2022

Join the Cullen & Big Paul Fan Club!

If you enjoyed the adventures of Cullen and Big Paul, why not join their fan club? You'll get early notice of new books, special offers, a monthly newsletter from the author, unique free content, invitations for discounts and more!

JOIN TODAY!

Tell others what you thought...

If you enjoyed this book, please leave a review on Amazon.

Or, you can buy more Cullen and Big Paul adventures here!

About the Author

You can learn more about Mark Farrer at www.markfarrer.com, like him on Facebook here or follow him on Twitter @mark_farrer.

Printed in Great Britain
by Amazon

43922549R00086